Aminatu's Spirit

Shirley Skyers-Thomas

INDULGENT INSIGHTS

AMINATU'S SPIRIT

Skyers-Thomas, Shirley

Aminatu's Spirit

ISBN 10: 0-692-89665-1

ISBN-13: 978-0-692-89665-5

PAPERBACK EDITION

DEDICATION

*TO MINE – I AM CONSTANTLY INSPIRED BY
YOUR SPIRIT. THANK YOU FOR ALLOWING ME
TO SEE YOU, AND SIMULTANEOUSLY SEE
MYSELF.
I AM GRATEFUL FOR THIS JOURNEY.*

WITH LOVE AND BLESSINGS,
Shirley

TABLE OF CONTENTS

PROLOGUE

The phone rang waking Mina from her nap on the couch. How she was able to nod off in the middle of the afternoon was beyond her. She scrambled around to find her phone in the mass of pillows that surrounded her. Disoriented, she looked around the room.

"Love, are you here? Oren?"

Mina shook her head waking herself up as her phone kept ringing.

"Hello?"

She tried her best to sound awake despite the dried drool that surrounded her mouth.

"Aminatu Blake?"

"This is."

"This is Detective Scott Toure from the city police department. Can you come downtown?"

"Downtown? To the police station? I don't understand. Am I in some sort of trouble? I don't even know where the station is."

Mina was completely awake and alert now. Dazed by the conversation, she stood up quickly—so quickly she nearly lost her footing.

"With all due respect, Detective Toure is it? I'm not coming down to the station without more information. Matter of fact, let me have my husband call you. He's Senator Blake and I know he'd want to know what's going on here."

The other line was silent. Seconds that registered like hours passed with no response from the detective.

"Ma'am, this is about your husband. I'm sorry but there's been an … incident. I truly suggest you come speak with us."

✠✠

CHAPTER 2: BEGINNINGS

Oren Blake met the love of his life on the campus of NYU.

"I'll love you for lifetimes, my queen," he'd often share with his beautiful girlfriend.

"Oh, I'm a queen now. I've been promoted!" she always responded cocking her head back as she laughed.

And like clockwork, Oren countered with the same phrase: "You're always my queen, my goddess, my love. I knew that the moment I laid eyes on you."

Oren was a Rhodes Scholar at NYU. He had a brilliant mind and a bright future. When they met, Oren was finishing a dual-graduate program in international politics and international business. Aminatu was a senior in NYU's undergrad business school but had already been accepted to the MBA program. Always ingenious and fiscally conscientious, Oren worked his way through the graduate program as a teaching assistant. Similarly, Aminatu was driven and no nonsense when it came to education. From the onset, Oren and Aminatu gravitated to each other.

Filling in for a fellow TA, Oren agreed to cover a senior thesis class. The professor was known to be hard to the point of unwavering. Oren slipped in late and took a seat right beside the door. The small lecture hall was jammed with nearly seventy students clinging carefully to each word Professor Brumley said. A few of them anxiously rubbed their temples or played with their hair as he spoke. Others tried to follow intently as they fiddled with their books. Oren chuckled to himself at their misfortune as he glanced around the room. But then he saw her. Aminatu was seated in the back of the room, seemingly oblivious to her classmates or much else. Reclined in the chair, holding a notebook, Aminatu jotted down notes every few seconds. She nodded with Professor Brumley and mouthed a few phrases in concert with him. Oren was immediately struck.

Mina, as Aminatu was known, was beautiful and unspoiled by her adopted Western lifestyle. Fashionable but simple. Radiant in her ethnic authenticity. Her skin was flawless: dark like chocolate from the cacao bean. Her hair, kept very short in those days, was the perfect combination of coils, curls, and slightly untamed locks. She moved with an air of confidence, but her vulnerability was apparent. Oren's eyes followed her profile; he couldn't stop staring. Perhaps it was her beauty. Then again, it could have been her confidence that separated her from her classmates. Either way, Oren felt there was a certain aura that surrounded her. It drew him in.

He eyed her from head to toe. He didn't know her, but he was sure he needed to. Although he never considered himself the romantic type, he immediately relished the idea of making her his forever. Embarrassed to admit it, he was sure he wanted to get to know this precious specimen of God much better. His eyes lingered until Aminatu caught him staring at her. She smiled, a little nervously at first until it became obvious he would not avert his eyes.

Class was over and Oren was intent on meeting her. He jumped up to climb the stairs at the rear of the lecture hall, just as Professor Brumley cleared his throat.

"Young man, are you filling in for Michael?"

Oren turned quickly to address the older man, hoping to move the conversation along.

"Yes, sir, I am."

Professor Brumley remained quiet as he searched the ceiling with his eyes. Students from the next class started filing into the lecture hall and a steady throng of students moved in and out of the space. Oren glanced up and down the rows and didn't see Aminatu. He rocked back and forth on his heels as the professor's eyes darted from one corner of the ceiling to the other.

"Great!" the professor finally said. "I have some assignments for you."

***

Every moment since the senior thesis class, Aminatu couldn't help but think about the handsome TA. She fantasized and ruminated to the point that her stomach was in knots. She wasn't sure when she would see him again. She couldn't have guessed that it'd be the next day.

As it turned out, Oren's graduate program organized an international community mixer that he chaired. It was his responsibility to ensure the comfort and contentment of the attendees, and from the looks of things, he took his job seriously. International students and faculty mingled and enjoyed an abundant spread of authentic fare.

The steel drums rang out to usher in a new song and, unintentionally, to welcome Aminatu. She made her way through the entrance, past the food, and directly to a spot that was seemingly waiting for her. She moved effortlessly to the ring of the steel drums and the heavy bass that kept it all together. Her body was made to move. Mina's hips welcomed each beat of the music. It washed over her as she swayed and bopped up and down. She closed her eyes and became the music. Soon, she was the focal point of the floor. When she finally opened her eyes, she was surprised to see she was the only one dancing. Panic-stricken, she dropped her head and searched the floor for solace. The moment she heard the next drumbeat, Oren was right there, matching her step for step, hand on her waist, keeping tempo with her as she began to glide again.

"Hello, my queen. What is your name?"

"They call me Mina."

She was so glad to see her knight coming to her rescue that she inched closer to him, allowing their bodies to unite on the dance floor, their faces beaming the whole time.

Shortly thereafter, their fascination and admiration with each other became a love affair that neither could ignore. Inseparable, they stayed hip to hip and in lockstep. Right after Mina completed her master's in business, they jumped the broom. Literally.

Mina pledged, "As long as I live … and in the spirit realm also … I will love you, my king."

✠✠

CHAPTER 3: GUESS WHAT?

"Baby, guess what?"

Oren rushed through the door to their two-story condo. Mina appeared at the top of the stairs looking exceptionally radiant for no reason at all.

"Tell me, love! Tell me everything." Mina smiled sweetly and beckoned for him to come to her.

"Well, all the junior senators, myself and Greg and Rick, have been invited to the international summit on climate change. You'll never guess where it's being held this year!"

Oren was so visibly excited, Mina found him irresistible. Joining in the celebration, she grew excited too and started to dance and clap.

"Where?"

"JA-MAI-CA! And guess who's coming with me?"

"Whoo! Yes? Me, baby? Yes!"

Oren grabbed his wife and spun her around.

"You, me, sun, sand, music, and food. Oh my God. It's been so long since I've been back. Not since Granddaddy's funeral."

Mina and Oren danced in earnest to the music that they shared, but only in their heads and hearts.

Her husband's rise in politics was a source of excitement and surprise. He was committed to the city and his constituents and was dedicated to doing the best job he could. He had made so many strides in such a short time. In six years, he had risen through the ranks and was now the city's youngest senator. Mina doted on his every move; she stood with him at every event, every awards banquet, every fundraiser, every symposium, every summit. She was proud of the man he was. Deep inside, she took great pride in her contribution to his development.

Her support of his career was not to the exclusion of her own. After many years in the trenches of private-sector finance, Mina had finally gotten her shot at the big league. She had just been appointed the CFO for a nonprofit focusing on developing women in business.

Together, Mina and Oren were definitely the power couple to watch. They worked hard, played hard, and loved hard. Jamaica for a few days was exactly what they both needed.

✠ CHAPTER 4: JAMAICA

"Baby, I'm so glad you booked the few days after the summit. Now, we get to enjoy ourselves. Five more days!"

Mina flopped on the king-sized bed in their suite. Not to be outdone, Oren took a running leap landing square on top of her.

"Oren!"

They both laughed uncontrollably until tears came from their eyes.

Mina and Oren spent the next few days touring the island and eating everything that came across their plates: boiled dumplings, fried plantains, oxtail, goat, callaloo, fish soup. Nothing was refused. For every dish, Oren gave a story of why it was his favorite.

"You know, Mummy taught me how to knead dumpling when I was just a little youth."

"Wow. Aunty Rose used to have us little ones pick the callaloo so she could clean it and cook it up."

"Yo… Granddaddy used to have chickens. He had a goat that…"

Mina could've complained about Oren's musings, but he did it so adorably, she didn't dare. She loved him and his heritage.

"Two more nights, my love." Mina sprawled over their king-sized bed. "This is almost our last night in paradise."

"Yeah, I know. Can't believe how fast it went. We'll have to do it again." Oren rubbed her feet as he spoke. "Or maybe next time, we can find your paradise on the other side of the world."

"Ooh! Now that's a plan. We'll go." Mina bubbled with excitement.

"Yep," Oren continued. "Wherever you want, whenever you want. But as for tonight, what do you want to experience?"

Mina sat up now that Oren piqued her interest.

"We haven't gone to your dad's hometown yet," she said. "You must see your grandmother. And it's close, right? Let's go there tonight. Didn't you tell me the best dancing spot is right there in town? Maybe we could get some dancing in."

"Done!" Oren high-fived his wife and she flopped back down on the bed.

Oren and Mina made their way there with a hired car. Pulling up in the dirt driveway of Mother Blake's home, the neighborhood came out to meet them. Mother Blake lived in a small house in the smaller north side of the parish of Saint James.

Kids ran down the street to greet them and to see who Mother Blake's people were.

✠✠

CHAPTER 5: MOTHER BLAKE

"Woye! Look ere! A mi baby dis?"

Mother Blake slowly rose to her feet from the hard-backed chair on the exposed veranda. Quickly scooting out of the car, Oren rushed up the dirt path. He trotted to the waiting matriarch of his family with open arms. Carefully he inserted himself within his grandmother's grasp. She was a large woman but short compared to Oren's six-foot-three frame.

They hugged for what felt like an hour to Mina, as she stood with the hot sun burning the back of her neck.

Mother Blake said repeatedly, "Mi boy come ome." Tears streaked her face and she stepped back to take a good long look at her grandson.

Mina stepped out of the driveway and approached the porch where the two were embracing. She walked awkwardly on the gravel and dirt path and smoothed her dress while wiping the sweat from her palms.

"A who dis pretty likkle ting?" Mother Blake said, clapping her hands slowly.

"Mumma," Oren said, "this is my Mina."

Mother Blake took Mina's hands in hers and kissed them. Mina allowed the tears that she was holding back to flow. Mother Blake led them into the house making sure not to let go of either's hand.

Children ran up and down the street. Some played ball and tag with each other. A few curious little ones peeped in the makeshift windows of Mother Blake's modest home. Neighboring adults stopped in to look at the sight, marveling at the couple sitting inside. Some paid close attention to the unfolding events. Others went about their business, oblivious to the reunion that had been years in the making.

It was rare that Mother Blake had company and allowed them to enter her property. It was even rarer that she was in such a relaxed state in the presence of visitors. But then again, these two were not visitors.

Evening started to fall. Mother Blake insisted they stay for a meal. Taken by Mother Blake's kindness and genuine affinity for her grandson, Mina pushed Oren to accept. Without too much protest, Oren helped Mother begin the meal. Mina made herself comfortable and returned to the veranda. She gazed at the sky; the sun had begun to set and the first glimpses of night were visible. The air was heavy and carried the scent of burning wood. Faintly in the distance, she heard the sound of heavy drums accompanying reggae music. She moved in response to the music, tilting her head slightly, finding her rhythm. The music soothed her and she closed her eyes. After a few moments, she lifted her hands letting them also find movement.

Mina drifted off into her own thoughts, carried away by the consistent drumbeat. Interrupting her thoughts and dance, a sharply dressed older man limped from the road up to Mother Blake's porch. His cane assisted his uneven gait.

"Hello and good night, miss," he said.

Mina delayed her response as she caught her breath. "Good evening, sir," she stammered.

"You must be Mother Blake's people."

"Yes. My husband is her grandson."

"Oh, yeah? Nice, nice, nice. I see you dance like us. You have the Yoruba rhythm. You are also Yoruba people, right? You must be Ifa?"

"Yoruba people? No, sir. Us? No. Wait. As in *my* people? No. We are Christians..." Mina continued to stammer until the older man laughed.

Mina was instantly flustered by the way she responded or rather by her appearance of complete and utter confusion.

"Yeah? So, you're not Ifa? All right. So, family of the High Priestess does not take to the Orisha? All right."

Mina furled her eyebrows and spoke softly. Her voice was barely above a whisper. "What do you mean the High Priestess, sir?" Her voice cracked as she said, "Orishas?"

The old man started to laugh. He cocked his head to one side and placed his hand on his hip.

"Oh, yes, my dear. Mother Blake is the Most Reverent Priestess of Yemaya. She is a mother of all mothers. Just as the goddess mother Yemaya is as well. As for the Orisha, you've got to learn your history. Orisha was here before we were. Before all of this"—he gestured around himself—"they were."

"So, you mean..." Mina sat upright becoming instantly enthralled with the old man's information.

Oren entered the front porch and placed a light hand on his wife's shoulder. "Dinner is ready, my queen."

"Eh eh, queen!" the old man remarked. "Are we in the presence of royalty? What is your name, miss?"

Suddenly very self-conscious and shy, Mina took a deep breath. "My name is Aminatu Cisse Blake."

"Aminatu. Beautiful. A beautiful name for a beautiful queen. You truly are a queen."

"She is my queen," responded Oren with a wide smile.

"Yes, I'm sure. But Aminatu is a queen in her own right. You know that part of your history, right?"

So as not to appear perpetually ignorant, Aminatu nodded her head up and down vigorously.

Mother Blake called from inside the house, "Come. Come baby, come."

Oren took Mina's hand. "Come, my love. Mumma calls."

Dinner was a traditional Jamaican spread. Mina was becoming very fond of the culinary delights. Oren ate each meal as though he was inhaling the very life-giving nectar he seemed to crave. There was distinct satisfaction on his face as he ate this evening. Seated at a table in the backyard, they dined in the open air. It was peaceful and quieter than Mina had ever experienced. Yet still, she felt a busy undercurrent probably due to the many animals busying themselves around her. Nevertheless, she took it all in and finished her meal just as the faint drumming she'd heard earlier began again.

Mother Blake rose slowly, this time with Oren right by her side functioning as her walking stick. She beckoned for Mina to come with her. Mother Blake made her way to the front of the house with Oren's help. Pausing for Mina to catch up and take her other arm, Mother Blake led the trio down the street. The strong scent of mint salves from her hands permeated the air. The fragrance was so strong, Mina could taste it. The combination of food, bodies, and mint hit her all at once. It was completely overbearing yet oddly comforting.

✠✠

CHAPTER 6: THE DANCE

As Mother moved through the road, her neighbors peeked their heads through window frames and cracks in doors. The excitement slowly started to build with low rumblings on the once silent street. Mother's movements caused a great stir as many quickly slipped out their homes to walk with her. The drumming became louder - this time with no reggae behind it, no instruments — just raw. One single drum. Mother Blake continued to walk. Slowly. The farther she walked, the more folks came out in response to her silent beckoning. What was one drum had now become two: speaking to each other in a call and response, mimicking and releasing the sound of each other.

Mother walked slowly, rhythmically. Neighbors who gathered to walk with her started to grunt. With each step, the grunts grew louder and more intense. Those who had been reluctant to join the movement were instantly recruited. It seemed that the entire street and surrounding ones were marching to the drum enticements. Synchronized movement was at its peak. The younger ones incorporated a hop to their march. Back, forth, back, forth. Amazingly the grunts hit the varying beats of the drums. No words were uttered, but it was the most beautiful melodic compilation that Mina had ever heard. The group wasn't making great strides or headway as they walked, but that was obviously not the intention.

Mother Blake stopped in her tracks. Shaking Oren off from her left side, she shook free of Mina as well. She clapped to the one beat of the loudest drum. A sway from side to side was the signal. She was suddenly very stable on her feet. Her socked feet shifted in small but sure steps. Her claps became more deliberate although still fairly soft.

Within moments, the heartbeat-like sounds of the drums took over the small throng that gathered in the street. The drums became louder. This time, a chorus of drums was easily identified. At least six separate drumbeats were heard. Emerging from a hidden side alley, the drums led a group of even more marching, hopping, clapping neighbors.

Before Mina realized what was happening, the group nearly doubled in size with Mother Blake at the center of a drum circle. Women in intricate head wraps started to dance in place. The drums were beat in unison and the entire congregation started to dance. Organized and slightly reserved, the dancing became more choreographed. The grunts moved into a guttural chorus of a song Mina did not understand.

The drums signified a change.

Boom. Bop, Bop!

Boom. Bop, Bop!

Mother Blake's folks abandoned the choreography and let go. The drums beat faster. Impulsively. The drummers were each in their own worlds, called to drum for simultaneously selfish and global reasons. As the drummers led the congregation in individualized dance, the spirit of the drum took over. Without concern for each other, the congregation danced hard with true abandon. Women screamed and convulsed as they danced. Men moved as warriors. Some were light on their feet, raising their knees high; others were heavy with slow, calculated movements.

Mina and Oren couldn't resist the release that happened as they held hands and closed their eyes. In love with each other and the culture, their spirits soared. Mina shook her head and relaxed her shoulders.

Oren seemed to be the first of the two to let go of his westernized self for just a moment. As the drums were struck, the roar of the crowd grew. His body went in deeper. Shaking. Moving. Head down. Heavy movements. As the drums intensified, he let go of Mina's hand and began to dance around. Oren left the ground ever so slightly. His shoes still connected with the ground. He dragged his feet back and forth.

Mother Blake remained in the center of the dance and drum circle. She shifted her weight to each foot but was careful not to exaggerate her movements.

Mina took to the periphery of the dance circle. She let the drums intoxicate her to the point that she left the center where Mother Blake and Oren were. Mina found the lead drummer at the corner of the circle as his drum beckoned her closer. She danced with her hips, her arms and allowed her feet to do whatever they desired. In moments, she was arm in arm with the drummer, only allowing him one hand for the Bop! Mina didn't care. She wound her hips, kicked her legs, and let out a guttural hoop herself. After a few minutes of the dance, the wailings of the women turned to tears.

✠

CHAPTER 7: THE SPIRIT FALLS

Bop!

The drums indicated yet another change.

Mother Blake stood in front of her people. "Hear dis, my people. Feel the love of our Mother Goddess Yemaya."

Mother Blake clapped and the congregation clapped as well. "Tek it! Hold it! Keep it!"

Mother Blake went on speaking for a short while in the midst of the tributes, the wailings, and tears.

Mina did not stop dancing. Now coordinating her movement to the spoken word, she felt an energy embrace her. It entered her body and twirled within her. For just a brief moment, her body was no longer hers. The energy originated from her belly and radiated to the rest of her. She spun and leaped in a way she had never done before. Just as she thought she was without the energy, it danced again within her, sparking her to convulse, raising a passion within her that was uniquely hers.

Oren was still near the center of the circle. He continued the heavy-footed dance coupled with tears and wailings himself. It felt like the congregants danced under the stars and on the open road for many hours. Once they finally allowed the energy and spirit to calm them, many of the parish folks returned solemnly to their homes.

Sweaty and hot, Oren and Mina found each other at the conclusion of the drum circle. He gently grabbed her body and held her close as her heart beat wildly against his chest. Weakened by the activity, Mina nearly collapsed. Oren, on the other hand, appeared strengthened by the experience. As he held Mina close, her essence comingled with his. She raised her head from his shoulder and stared deeply into his eyes. Through their gazes, they completed the transference of energy, sealing the covenant that already existed.

"Come, my queen." Oren carried Mina down the short dirt path back to Mother Blake's home. The old man from earlier led Mother Blake by the arm down the road, walking steadily, step by step with his cane.

✠✠

CHAPTER 8: LEAVING ST. JAMES

The following morning, Mother Blake was up early preparing a hearty breakfast. By the time Mina and Oren rose, a lovely meal awaited them. Mother Blake seemed even more rejuvenated than the previous day. Her steps were lighter and her energy was high. There appeared to be renewed life infused in the woman well in to her eighties.

She chatted to them in Jamaican patois as she fluttered about the kitchen making sure her grandson and granddaughter were content. She told them of all the comings and goings of her neighbors. She recounted stories of Oren's grandfather, her husband, who had died a number of years ago. It was obvious she was in great spirits.

Nervous to broach the subject, Oren took a deep breath.

"Mumma. What *was* that last night?"

Mother Blake stopped what she was doing and turned slowly to face the couple.

"Last night, mi dear, was de life force come out inna de dance."

She explained a bit more about how the drum circle and dance were prayer and praise for her people.

Oren was still hesitant to ask about how she was the High Priestess and especially how he didn't know. Realizing that he wouldn't get all of his questions answered, he left that alone. Mina remained quiet as well.

Time moved quickly. Before they realized it, it was late afternoon and the hired car was back to pick them up. Just as they had come a mere day earlier, they left. An even greater throng of people gathered at Mother Blake's house for their send-off. Mother Blake was in the midst laughing and smiling, genuinely joyful for her family. She hugged Oren until they swayed and danced together.

"Mi love you a know. Love you, love you, love you."

"Yes, Mumma," Oren nearly whispered. "I love you too."

After one last squeeze, Mother Blake let go. Mina went in for a quick hug and Mother Blake held her affectionately.

"You are strong, ya hear? Strong."

Amid hugs from strangers alike, they left.

✠✠

CHAPTER 9: THE PRECINCT

Mina sat in front of Detective Toure at the downtown police station. She'd somehow arrived at the station, but couldn't recall anything after receiving his phone call. She sat still—expressionless and numb. Detective Toure inched a paper cup of liquid closer to her. At a loss, he stood and disappeared into a back room for a few minutes. He slunk back and slid into his chair, unnoticed and unacknowledged.

"Mrs. Blake? Again, I'm so sorry for your loss. Your husband did a lot for this city."

Mina did not respond. Sitting motionless she appeared to not even be breathing.

"Do you want one of our officers to take you home? You can come whenever you're up for it to identify the…the…"

"No," Mina whispered. "I'll do it now. I won't come back here."

Taken aback, Detective Toure scrambled to his feet and offered a shaky, outstretched hand to Mina. Robotically, she accepted it and was guided down a long corridor to the site of her husband's body. The detective held her hand firmly as he led her around corners and down a short set of stairs.

Mina watched as he methodically removed the covering from Oren's face.

A wave of pain attacked her body. Holding her stomach, she felt the sensation of multiple knives piercing her organs. Screaming in pain, she doubled over. Her wails became louder and louder. Waves of torture pierced her soul. Instantaneously, her heart rate dropped and her head pounded. Tormented by the sound of inconceivable noises in her head, she gripped her skull and tried to steady herself. She was unable to control any bodily functions, her nose gushing bright red blood right before she fell to the linoleum floor. A puddle of urine amassed around her as she lay.

Her body jumped as if she were having a nightmare. Mina opened her eyes to find herself on a hard wooden bench. Detective Toure was replacing the smelling salts in a med bag. He removed the cold compress that was on her forehead.

"We'll get you home, Mrs. Blake. Is there someone who can stay with you tonight?" he asked.

Mina shook her head "no" and instantly regretted it. The pounding resumed and she lay her head back down on the bench.

"Officer, can you give me a hand please?" Detective Toure beckoned to one of the female officers.

"I'm taking Mrs. Blake home. You're riding shotgun, Snow?"

The officer winked and nodded her head.

Mina was drenched in urine and blood and completely helpless. She mumbled a few words incoherently as she leaned on the door frame waiting for the officers. Before long, the officer and detective were outside Mina's complex. With muffled speech that was mostly unintelligible, she directed them to her keys then somehow found herself on her couch.

Mina saw the detective speaking to her but she heard nothing. The officer riffled through her bathroom cabinet and produced a bottle of ibuprofen. She placed that and a glass of water on the side table beside where Mina lay. Detective Toure scribbled a handwritten note on an envelope and left it under the glass. They let themselves out and left Mina to madness.

***

The doorbell rang. Mina shuffled to the front door and checked the peephole. Her body raged with pain. Simple movements made her muscles ache. Opening the door slightly, Mina peered through the tiny crack. Detective Toure stood there waiting patiently.

"Yes?" she said. Her voice was hoarse and barely audible.

"Mrs. Blake, it's me Detective Toure from the precinct. I have your car keys. Your car is parked outside. Right there if you care to take a look."

Mina opened the door a bit wider. The morning's sun flooded the alcove where she stood. She lifted her arm to shield her eyes. Still wearing yesterday's clothes, Mina reeked of many unpleasant odors. Her skin was pale and her eyes were nearly swollen shut.

"What time is it?" she asked.

"Ten of ten. Too early? I apologize…" Detective Toure stuttered.

"Listen," Mina whispered, "I really don't remember anything that happened last night. Why do you have my car? And who are you again?"

She snatched her keys out of his opened hand.

Detective Toure recounted the evening, being careful not to recap that Oren Blake had been killed in a car crash. He restated how he and Officer Snow had brought her back home but left her car at the precinct.

Mina cracked the door wider and looked the detective up and down. As she moved slightly, she started to swoon a bit. Detective Toure reached out for her before she collapsed again. She slumped into his chest. He hoisted her up and led her to the couch, closing the door behind them.

Leaning her head on the wall behind her, Mina spoke slowly and distinctly. "Start from the beginning and tell me everything again." Her words were heavy as she fought for the air to release them. She reached for the ibuprofen bottle that lay open on its side and popped a few in her mouth, swallowing painfully.

"Okay, Mrs. Blake" — the detective took a deep breath followed by a few short ones — "your husband, Oren, was found at the scene of what appeared to be a rollover on I-95 at approximately two o'clock Saturday, yesterday afternoon. Upon quick inspection of his vehicle, it is consistent with loss of control of the vehicle followed by quick impact with the guardrail. The speed at which he was likely traveling propelled him over the guardrail and down the embankment. It seemed that he wasn't wearing his seat belt, so he was thrown from the car. There was a small fire as a result. This all occurred on the east side and the rain made the scene that much more treacherous. We'll be conducting a full investigation."

Mina whimpered continually but without the physical suffering she experienced the previous day.

"My husband is a very experienced and careful driver. This doesn't make sense. This doesn't make sense…"

Each word Mina uttered was steeped in pain. The detective sat rigidly. She spoke in hushed tones and he rubbed his forehead in confusion. Perhaps he couldn't hear her and perhaps that was best.

"Mrs. Blake, our team will be doing everything we can to piece together the events so that they make sense and we all understand what happened."

"Well I can tell you right now — *that* didn't happen. And I really don't care if you understand." Mina bit her lip as tears poured down her cheeks again. "Oren is careful, was careful," she said woefully, "and he would never travel without his seat belt on. He wouldn't speed in the rain either. He's kind of an old man in that regard." Mina smiled to herself obviously recalling a sweet memory. "Especially not on the highway."

"I do understand, Mrs. Blake. Our team will be working diligently to put the details together. Before I leave, is there anyone I can call for you? Shall I make your family aware?"

Mina nodded up and down slowly as hot tears again rolled down her cheeks.

✠✠

CHAPTER 10: NIGHTTIME VISITATION

Mina barely moved from her position on the couch once the detective left. Night came quickly and the physical pain returned. She was plagued with intense, gut-wrenching pain. Her skin crawled and she felt a stabbing pain in her stomach. She vomited until nothing more could be expelled. She tried to lie down in the bed, but Oren's scent on their sheets was torture. In the midst of her violent tears, she felt the gush of blood escape from her nose again. She tried to make it to the bathroom only a few feet away. When she stood, her head throbbed and pounded, which brought on vertigo, something she had never experienced before. Mina crashed to the floor, banging her head as she went down. Sharp pains stabbed her chest, making it difficult to breathe; she gasped every few minutes. She knew she was going to die. *For the best*, she thought. Struggling, she drew a faint breath.

"I can't do this without you, Oren."

Mina released the little strength she had left.

The smell of the outside air awakened her. Lights blinded her as the sound of sirens went off consistently. A large woman pushed the stretcher she was on into an ambulance where another EMT waited to receive her. Mina tried to move her head only to find that she was constricted by a neck brace, her body secured tightly by straps. She was bloody and her shirt had been cut off of her. Covered only by a thin sheet, she felt the coolness of the evening air whip around her. A man spoke to her as he shoved a light in her face to check her eyes. Blinking profusely, Mina closed her eyes again. The man continued talking but she heard nothing.

She felt pulsation followed by the warmth of a hand on hers. The hand squeezed hers and its owner spoke softly to her. Mina couldn't make anything out and barely had the energy to open her eyes.

With one eye opened, she saw a gorgeous woman kneeling beside her in the back of the ambulance. Her lips moved but Mina still heard nothing.

"Candy," Mina whispered with tears in her eyes.

***

The Blakes had been transplants to the area; therefore, no family was called to the hospital. Mina had friends, only one of whom she was very close to. Candace Kone. Thankfully, the detective had contacted Candace about Oren's death earlier that day and she rushed to Mina's home as soon as she could.

Candace told the emergency personnel that she knew something was wrong because she saw Mina's car but couldn't get her to answer the door.

Once at Metro General Medical Center, Candace did not leave Mina's side. Quickly through triage, Mina was taken to an emergency room and hooked up to a host of monitors. They ran a battery of tests. They checked her heart, her organ function, and especially her head considering the huge gash she now had. Although the attending doctor checked on Mina regularly, Candace fretted the whole night. Mina remained conscious but did not speak to anyone other than Candace. She moaned on and off.

The attending ER doctor peeked her head in the room and announced, "Everything has come back negative. I'm clearing Aminatu for discharge. The nurse will be in shortly to help you both wrap up."

Candace stopped the doctor as she was about to leave the room again. "Will she be okay tonight?" Candace asked. "What's going on with her?"

"She is suffering from acute traumatic anxiety further compounded by her fall. The manifestation is rarely as severe as your friend's, but it's been known to occur."

"Are you saying that all this was a simple anxiety attack?" Candace asked, frowning.

"At its base level, yes. But this was no simple attack. Whatever troubled her nearly took her life. Our psyche is a powerful thing and not to be taken likely."

"I'll take care of her. We're all we got," Candace said.

***

By the time Monday rolled around, Mina was fully under the care of her best friend. Candace had come with a huge suitcase and settled quickly into the guest room. She was in for the long haul.

Candace was an entrepreneur, working in the city as a highly sought after interior designer. She and Mina had met in college when they both were in the MBA program. They had so much in common — their backgrounds and ethnicity — it was no wonder they took to each other instantly.

In the days following Mina's loss, Candace was her right hand and pledged to stay as long as she was needed.

Candace was as distraught as Mina about Oren's death. Between the two of them, they informed the world of his passing. News traveled quickly between countries and continents. With Candace's help, Mina planned a lovely homegoing that was fit for her king.

Days after the funeral, Mina was still oblivious and instead operated completely on autopilot. She acted out of routine and habit. She was distracted, and it was occasionally intentional. She was so wrapped up in the preparation and execution of Oren's funeral arrangements, she hadn't processed the circumstances of his death.

Candace peeked her head around the living room corner to address her. Mina looked off in the distance and moaned softly.

"Sweetie, you can't live like this." Candace started to tidy the room. She picked up pictures and papers that were strewn about the floor. "Time to get up. How about you take a shower and I'll finish up in here?" Candace asked.

Mina grunted and made small efforts to stand.

Candace scurried about, picking up, organizing, and arranging the home that Mina watched slip into disarray.

"Here, sis. You want this?"

Candace handed Mina the piece of paper that had sat on the side table since Detective Toure placed it there. It had now yellowed and some of the pen ink had run.

Detective Scott Toure 347-481-9235. Cell

Mina took the scrap of paper and fingered it for a few seconds. Moments later, she dialed the number.

"Hello? Detective Toure? This is Aminatu Cisse Blake. I have a few questions about my husband's death."

***

Mina sat in the booth at the coffee shop, nervously playing with her cup. Spinning it in a circle and twirling the paper napkins offered her some solace. She didn't notice the detective slide in across from her until he cleared his throat.

"Mrs. Blake?"

Startled, Mina tipped her cup over spilling coffee on the table.

"Oh no! So sorry!" she stammered.

"Don't be." Detective Toure grabbed a handful of napkins and sopped up the mess. He waved a waitress over and asked for another coffee for Mina and one for himself.

"So, as you requested, I gathered the information that our department now has."

Mina didn't look up from the table. "Okay."

Detective Toure kept on. "Upon a detailed investigation of Mr. Blake's vehicle, it seems that there was something faulty with his electrical panel and the fuel filter flange in his Mercedes."

"What? What do you mean?" Mina raised her head to stare in the detective's face.

"Okay, so you know how cars are controlled by their electrical panels? Well, something was wrong with Oren's...I mean...Mr. Blake's. It may have been the sole cause of the problem, ultimately contributing to the loss of control. Also, there was a fluid leak that was found in the fuel filter."

Detective Toure was quiet as he stared at the wall behind Mina. His eyes dashed across the wall and he mouthed a few words.

"Now that I think about it there was an excessive leak that we found on the highway. Whoa...hold on one sec."

Detective Toure turned away from Mina as he made a call.

"Snow, what was the status of the vehicle check in the Blake case."

He paused for a few seconds.

"Yeah...uh huh...yeah."

Turning again even farther into the booth and away from Mina, he continued to speak. "Is that right? Oh my God. Gotcha."

Hanging up, Detective Toure seemed to have lost some of the color in his face. "Mrs. Blake, it appears that your husband's car was tampered with in a number of ways. One of which likely caused the fire. We're looking into the possibility that his brake lines were cut."

Mina cocked her head to one side, tears streaming down fast and furious. "So are you saying…"

"Yes, Mrs. Blake. I am. This is now a homicide investigation."

Detective Toure promised to be in touch in the next day or two with conclusive reports on Oren's murder.

That night, Mina was unable to sleep. The Ambien that Candace had secured for her was doing nothing. She had no desire to rest. Her mind was spinning.

Murder. Murder. How?

Mina allowed her mind to focus back on the last solid block of time she'd had with Oren: Jamaica. The parish of Saint James. She recalled the weather, the food, and the enrapturing dance.

Without much effort, Mina heard the sound of the drums and was transformed yet again.

Boom! Bop! Boom! Bop!

Mina settled into that feeling again. She felt the core of her body stir. Her body moved and swayed mindlessly. She shuffled to the center of her bedroom floor and immediately felt something grab on to her hips. Dismissing it, Mina embraced her rhythm and started to dance. She shook her hips back and forth slightly and started to feel the fullness of the presence. As she moved, she felt a significant pressure transfer from her hips to the small of her back. It gripped her and enveloped her like a hug. She shifted, rocking back and forth to the drumbeat which she now heard clearly. As the drums intensified, so did Mina's dance. She spun and whipped and grunted in a muffle that sounded more like a whimper. She darted from one side of the floor to the other. She waved her arms above her, summoning whatever it was to come closer. Sweat poured from her forehead into her eyes, yet she kept dancing. Her legs felt heavy and her muscles ached but she felt the presence push her to continue.

The drumming stopped abruptly. Mina froze and felt the room spin about her. On the verge of falling, she started to sway. Instead of falling to the cold hardwood floor, she felt the cushion of her soft bedsheets under her head. She took a deep breath and filled her nostrils with the scent of faint sandalwood.

"Mmmm. Ahhh..." she said.

Mina took it all in with closed eyes. She was convinced that this would heighten the experience. A pressure and heaviness in her stomach moved to her chest and back to her stomach. Moments later, it went in deeper—permeating skin and layers of muscle, barely dodging organs, and getting right into her core.

Mina convulsed as the heat from the intrusion engulfed her. The very cells of her body pierced her as they burned with the intensity of flames. As she shook, Mina heard, "You are strong, ya hear? Strong." Over and over she heard this mantra and smelled the distinct scent of mint salve.

As the burning subsided, Mina was able to sit up in her bed. In the darkness, the presence crystallized to a profile. Unsure why she wasn't petrified, she continued to stare into the darkness. The profile took even greater shape and became an unmistakable man. Light filtered in as he spread his arms. Mina was taken aback by his regalia. He wore an expansive red-and-black covering that filled the entire floor of the room. Despite the abundance of his regal garments, the man was completely uncovered. The garments only served to highlight his towering profile. He radiated with an energy that mimicked light but was more intense than that.

Mina was not fearful but greatly intrigued.

Who are you? she thought.

"Me? You ask who I am, yet I know you," the figure spoke audibly. "Do you hear that? You hear the music? The drums. Ohhh…come! Let's dance."

The figure cast off his covering and moved intentionally around Mina's room. Each movement was calculated. He moved seductively but took no interest in her body. He came close to her; Mina felt an energy that she recognized. She sat, disinterested in doing anything but watching this majestic form circle her room in pure joy.

"Will you tell me? Who are you?" Mina pleaded.

"I can be whomever you desire."

Mina pouted, saddened.

The figure moved into a smaller state. In contrast to being broad, he became a man slightly larger than Mina. He rocked back on his heels and folded his arms across his bare chest. He spoke and words escaped, yet Mina felt only the essence of this great being.

"You feel me. You feel me deep within the cells of your heart, but more importantly, your soul knows me. Your spirit has seen me before."

"However, the true question is not who I am, but who you are."

He brushed up to Mina aggressively. He knocked her onto the bed. She lay flat. His essence hovered over her. She felt as if she was being held down lightly. A weight pinned her arms. Her body felt heavy. Her legs were chained without any apparatus. Mina squirmed although completely comfortable and safe.

"Dear, Queen. Your journey begins today. Until the next time. And if you really need it, I can oblige you. I am Eshu."

"Eshu...Eshu..." Mina repeated.

The more that Mina repeated his name, the more she loved it. She was overcome with emotion and started to cry. She embraced the feeling although she did not know why she was crying. She was far from sad in this moment. Nevertheless, her chest grew heavy with the feelings that inhabited her being.

Mina heard the drums resume their beats. Closing her eyes, she felt Eshu's essence release her. When she finally scanned the room, there was no evidence that anyone else was in the room with her. The scent of sandalwood remained as if a gentle reminder of her reality.

✢✢

CHAPTER 11: THE CAPITOL

Mina sat disengaged at the kitchen table across from her best friend.

"Sis, I'm here for you in any way. Do you want to talk about it?" Candace spoke earnestly with an air of concern.

Mina looked at Candace for the first time that morning, despite that they'd been in each other's presence for about an hour.

"Thanks, Candy. You've been a godsend."

Turning to face Candace squarely, Mina searched her face looking for something. "Candy, you ever feel…like *feel* stuff. Something you can't even explain?"

Candace softened her expression. "Absolutely, honey. You mean like loss? The same way I felt after Baba died. A significant void. Like my world crumbled around me."

Mina blinked her eyes and pursed her lips for a moment. "More than that, Candy. More than simple emotion. Like the center of your body is going to implode. Like…like…" Mina stammered.

Mina threw her head back, closed her eyes, and shook her head slowly. "What am I saying? Okay,

Candy." Mina exhaled deeply and blurted out, "Who is Eshu?"

Candace placed her fork down and leaned in to her friend, narrowing her eyes. "Eshu, Mina? Why? Eshu? Did something happen to you?" Her voice was a whisper. She stared at the ceiling and scrunched up her nose. "When I was little, my grandmother used to tell stories about the Orisha. Her favorite was Eshu-Elegbara. When she spoke, her eyes were always wide with excitement and fear. She kinda had that look right there," Candace said, circling Mina's face in the air.

"Orisha. There it is again..." Mina said.

Candace shot Mina a disapproving side eye. "Grandmother would tell us of how she regarded Eshu to be the one she felt closest to. She'd say she felt a stirring in her spirit that could only have been Eshu when she offered at the altar for him. Sometimes, she felt that he would let things happen to her, but it was for her own good. She said she loved him the best because there was always a learning in there somewhere. A learning. I guess that was Grandmother's thing."

Candace went on to tell Mina about the altars in her grandmother's house dedicated to the Orisha. Eshu, in particular, had been dominant in her home. There were others that Grandmother would make offerings and shrines for. The gracious Oshun was another one Grandmother loved and reveled in; yet, Candace explained, Eshu was her favorite.

Mina felt so ignorant. Why didn't she know? And how could she know? Who would teach her? She felt tightness in the pit of her stomach and took quick shallow breaths.

Candace waved her hands in the air dismissively. "But that was the older generation. You don't see me with any altars in my home. And you won't. Don't forget, Mina, we don't believe in that stuff. It's the myths that our grandparents believed. No place for that here. So, you never said, though. What happened to you? You have a dream or something?"

Biting her lip, Mina looked away. "No…Nothing. Just remembered that I heard that name before."

Mina felt the strong need to go to the capitol and collect Oren's belongings. It had been quite a while since the office informed her that she was welcome to gather his things. Today was the first day she felt up to it. Although Candace offered, she opted to go alone.

Mina was nervous and anxious as she shut off the engine in the municipal parking lot. Without any hesitation, she opened the door and briskly walked to the entrance of the capitol. She felt as if eyes were on her even as she walked. Trying to minimize the curve in her hips and the natural shake in her rear, she stiffened up. Almost robotic, she pushed open the office suite door amid stares and whispers.

Mina presented herself at the reception desk. The secretary appeared flustered as she tried to attend to her.

"Yes, ma'am, how, uh…um, may I help you?"

Mina cleared her throat and spoke softly yet clearly. "My name is Mrs. Blake. I'm here to accept my husband's belongings."

As she spoke, her shoulders softened and fell back straightening her stance. She appeared even taller and leaner than she already was. She relaxed on her feet and folded her hands in front of her.

The woman's face became flushed. "Oh! Yes, Mrs. Blake. We were so sorry to hear about Or…I mean your husband, Senator Blake. I really intended on going to the service, but…"

Mina felt a forceful hand on her shoulder.

A well-put-together gentleman stepped abruptly into the conversation. He was an exceptionally handsome man. From his shiny cuff links to his obviously tailored suit, he was definitely someone important to this office.

Considering that Mina knew most of Oren's colleagues from the many events she had attended right by his side, she was surprised by the new face.

He extended a hand in the most debonair manner. "I'm Senator Sam Kingsly. I had the pleasure of working with your husband, but from a distance. We knew each other and I respected him. His reputation is irrefutable in this office and in this city. He established a legacy that won't be forgotten. He was for the people and he will be sorely missed."

He flashed a megawatt smile and waited for Mina's response.

She nodded her head and mouthed her thanks.

"Can I escort you to his office?" he asked.

Senator Kingsly led Mina to the small office that Oren shared with another member of the Senate. She found a neatly packed box on the top of his desk. There was an array of books and a splattering of personal effects. Inside the cardboard box labeled *BLAKE*, Mina saw a number of familiar things. Tucked in the box on the side panel, there was a picture of Mina and Oren in Jamaica.

So happy, Mina thought.

The angle the picture was taken at made it look as if Mina and Oren had one single distorted body.

Oren loved that picture as he always referred to it as their inseparable body.

You know we're one, right? She heard Oren's voice in her head asking.

"Yes," Mina spoke out loud. "One."

A few of the less courageous individuals looked on from the doorway, but none approached her or attempted to speak to her.

Immediately very emotional, Mina grabbed the box and started to hustle out. Her purse fell off her shoulder and dropped to the floor. The contents spilled out and littered the hard tile. Keys, lotions, lipsticks, receipts, and a flurry of feminine products were scattered about. She tried to balance the box on her hip and pick up each of her items. Although she caused a stir, the handful of people that gathered around her just stood. Awkwardly, Mina picked up her things. The box on her hip started to feel heavy and she felt unbalanced. As she bent down to get the last of her items, the box tipped and crashed to the floor. On the verge of tears, she remained still and took one long deep breath. She breathed in a faint scent of sandalwood. Fighting tears, she relaxed her shoulders and neck.

"Mrs. Blake?"

Senator Kingsly bent beside her and handed her items from the purse and the box, including the framed picture that was now in a shattered frame.

Mina stared at the frame as he handed it over.

"May I take your box for you?"

She stood and composed herself, allowing Senator Kingsly to put the box back together and pick it up. On the walk to the car, she was silent.

Once they reached her car, he broke the silence. "I'm really sorry about the staff back there. Oren's death has been difficult for all of us."

He placed the box on the passenger seat. Mina put the shattered picture on top of the pile inside the box, which was now a disheveled mess. She remained poised and prepared to leave.

He offered her a business card. "If I can be of help during this difficult time."

Again, he flashed the wide smile, exposing most of his teeth.

✠✠

CHAPTER 12: VISITOR

Exhausted and still flustered, Mina secluded herself from Candace that evening. As she sat in the darkness of her bedroom, she recognized the familiar feeling of her mind clouding and her thoughts descending. Becoming more fatigued, she was filled with a sense of heaviness. In the distance, she heard the sound of drums. Within moments, her room was engulfed by the great presence; it manifested from nothing and revealed itself as the figure standing before her. Mina was mystified. She tried to catch her breath after realizing that she was barely breathing. She held her chest, feeling her heart race.

Towering and broad, Eshu entered. He danced and spun circles around the room, his essence increasing at every turn. Seemingly elated with himself and his performance, he was oblivious to Mina. She focused her attention on his regal nature and how he seemed to grow right in front of her. The drumming kept consistent rhythm with her heartbeat. Instead of growing louder this time, it remained a faint backdrop.

Eshu danced around Mina as she realized that she was now standing. He stopped to face her and moved in closely. He drew close enough for her to see him in earnest.

"Glorious," she whispered.

He arched his back and inhaled deeply, filling his being as he grew immense. He sucked the air from the room and held it inside himself. Mina held her breath. She was not sure what was about to happen but was convinced that it was going to be something. Terrified that she would miss this moment, she maintained her breath and remained fixated on him.

Eshu reached for Mina's hips and held her stable. With what seemed like his entire being, he unleashed the very breath that he had taken in—and let it go, directly into her belly. The breath that Mina was holding escaped immediately. She had the instinct to cough but was filled with air before she could. As he exhaled, Mina inhaled. Her lung cavities grew and her capacity to receive doubled. On her left flank, she felt a sensation. Unable to resist, Eshu permeated her body with his hand. She cried out, startled. Her cries turned to moans as she tolerated the discomfort. The more she moaned, the greater pleasure Eshu seemed to take in pursuing her body.

"Do you feel me?"

Eshu entered Mina deeper, now moving his forearm and shoulder into her body. Methodically, he placed his leg and half of his torso inside of her. He climbed in like Mina was his cloak. Eshu must have intended to slowly and deliberately encompass her entire body.

"Dear, Queen, do you feel me?" Eshu's voice echoed inside Mina's head.

Unable to respond, she shook intensely with her arms outstretched.

"*What* do I feel like? *Who* do I feel like?"

Eshu pushed himself entirely into Mina.

Her moans grew louder and turned into high-pitched screams. At the top of her lungs, she wailed, "What do you want?"

Candace threw open the bedroom door and fiddled with the lights.

"Eshu! What do you want from me!" Mina continued wailing. She spun in circles trying both to embrace him and shake him off. Neither attempt did anything but propel him deeper within her.

Candace rushed over to Mina who was standing, yet contorted in the center of her room. "Mina!"

Frightened, Candace tried to hold Mina together. With all that she had, Candace tried to force Mina's arms down, but Mina's strength was too much for her. With little effort, Mina resisted the hold causing Candace to fly across the room. Candace cowered in the corner where she felt somewhat safe.

Eshu continued to wreak havoc in the form of pain and pleasure inside Mina's body. She tried to scream but no sound could be released.

"You will never be the same, Queen," Eshu whispered. His words permeated Mina deeply. "You are very strong and powerful. Know me—know yourself. I will help you."

In an instant, Eshu removed himself completely from her. He left her body, but the lingering effects of his essence remained, as well as the light scent of sandalwood. Although Eshu's physical presence diminished, his greatness did not dissipate from the bedroom.

Mina checked her body and realized that she was all right. She was actually much more than all right.

Her body ached. Every muscle and cavity had been caressed. She felt different. Emotionally spent, she wanted to drop. But instead, her footing grew stronger and her stance more deliberate. She could have run around the block six times with the adrenaline that surged through her body.

Glancing at the corner of the room, Mina noticed Candace nearly hyperventilating.

"C'mon, sis." Mina extended a hand to pull her friend up. She lifted Candace quickly to her feet, as Candace grew even limper.

"Oh my God, Aminatu. Look at you," Candace wearily exclaimed and pointed at her friend.

Mina felt self-conscious for the first time that evening. "What, Candy?"

Candace stood and grabbed a handful of Mina's new locks. She fluffed them, laughing as she did. Mina had developed a head full of gorgeous long locks. They now reached the small of her back. Not only did she have beautiful long locks adorning her head, they were jeweled with perfect white cowrie shells.

Mina didn't look the same or feel the same.

✜

CHAPTER 13: THE OFFICE

"Hello, Mr. Readon. This is Aminatu Blake. Do you have a moment to discuss my e-mail request for a leave of absence?"

Mina spoke briefly to her boss and confirmed a six-week leave of absence. Feeling newfound freedom, she had a list of things she needed to accomplish. Six weeks was going to be tight, but she had to make it work.

Candace and Mina hadn't spoken after the previous night's events. Candace was up and out early. Although slightly concerned about the reason for her friend's early-morning exit, Mina was much more relieved that she didn't need to answer to her about last night. She figured she could deal with her later.

After choosing the outfit to make her look just right, Mina dressed and paid special attention to her makeup. She accentuated her already ravishing features. For a regular weekday at home, she was stunning.

She pushed open the heavy wooden double doors to Oren's home office. Everything was just as he had left it that Saturday morning before the accident. She had not been able to bring herself to even enter the room…until now. She carried the box she'd retrieved, nearly unsuccessfully, from the Senate office at the capitol.

Mina dropped it with a thud on the beautiful yet massive oak desk. She surveyed the room, recalling the stories of each item Oren had displayed prominently. She eyed his diplomas and degrees on the wall, reminding her instantly of NYU. Framed pictures covered his office virtually serving as his wallpaper: Mina's face was everywhere. Vacation, political events, big and small moments—their life was clearly portrayed in pictures.

She took out the files that were now stacked haphazardly on top of the box. Sifting through Oren's things, she made separate piles of his truly personal items and the work-related documents.

Her eyes caught a dingy manila envelope. She lifted it up, already unimpressed. There was no reason for anyone to take note of it. Flipping it over to examine it, Mina noticed that it had been opened and rather messily, glued back down. She held it up to the light to try to get a glimpse at the contents inside. All she was able to make out was a small, hard mass.

She opened the envelope neatly with extreme caution to avoid the same scrutiny that she was dishing out. A pendant-like charm dropped out. It had a curved half circle on the top connecting to a wave-like intricate pattern and was closed off with a half circle on the bottom. The base was a longer cylinder. Mina had never seen it before, but she felt connected to it. It was a beautiful bronze and well crafted. It was smooth to the touch, with some shiny parts that she couldn't stop running her fingers over. It was something that Mina would wear—in fact, it was just her style. She thought it could be a broach or lovely neck pendant.

Maybe Oren bought it for me as a present. He knew I'd love it, Mina thought.

She sat in Oren's plush rolling chair and admired the piece in her hands, continuing to rub it between her fingers. She threw her head back, letting her new locks cascade over the back of the chair. She took a deep breath in, reveling in Oren's scent. His skin, his cologne, his hair, the entire office smelled like him. Dolce & Gabbana was his favorite. As she rolled back in the chair, she saw Oren's black safe tucked under the desk. Without hesitation, Mina instinctively punched in the code. 0628. Their anniversary. The door popped open.

Off to the side, a little out of view, she saw the most ornately carved wooden box. It was evident that this item either cost significant money or a craftsman's time. She wondered why she had never seen this craftsmanship before. Oren never hid important things from her.

"Then again, maybe this wasn't that important," Mina said out loud.

But it was beautiful. However or from whomever, Mina concluded that she wanted it close to her. She went to flip it open and realized it was locked.

Intuitively, Mina placed her new pendant in the key hole and turned. She heard a click confirming that her secret box was now available. Excitedly she flew the top open, unsure of what she expected. Disappointed, she found nothing. It was nothing in her estimation. But in the middle of the smooth wooden surface, there was a USB flash drive. It was pretty typical looking and otherwise nondescript.

Curious, Mina rolled over to Oren's laptop, which sat neatly on the left corner of the desk. It powered up. Username: Oren Blake. Password: 0628.

The desktop wallpaper was the same photo of the two of them that had shattered. Mina smiled when she saw it. She slid the flash drive into the laptop and sat back expecting to view albums and albums of photos that Oren had taken.

PASSWORD PROTECTED flashed on the screen.

The small words puzzled her.

The opportunity to enter the password was below it, so like clockwork, Mina entered 0628.

PASSWORD INVALID

What? Mina thought.

She typed in their entire anniversary: month, day, and year this time.

PASSWORD INVALID

Mina furled her brows and stared at the screen. She likely only had one more attempt before she was locked out; she had no idea what that would entail. She touched her stomach noticing that it was slightly warm...warmer than the rest of her body.

She hunched over the desk and typed again.

A-M-I-N-A-T-U

The light on the drive flashed and the hourglass icon came up.

Documents opened immediately and scattered the screen. Mina blinked feverishly trying to understand what she was seeing.

She saw the consistent heading: *Senate Confirmation Hearing*. There was a plethora of documents with that same heading. She wasn't sure what she was looking at, however, she saw yet another consistent name: *Committee Chair — Sam Kingsly*.

Confused by why Oren kept this under lock and key, Mina dug into the documents.

✠✠

CHAPTER 14: UNIVERSITY ABUSE

After a few moments of reading, Mina determined that Attorney Ibra Marcus was up for confirmation as the state's attorney general.

Under normal circumstances, this would have been of little to no interest to Mina. However, still plagued by the fact that this particular information was hidden under lock, key, and passwords, she was determined to figure it out.

Oren was known to be thorough in his dealings: work and personal. Mina was not surprised to find files and files of research done in preparation for the confirmation hearing.

As a junior senator, having only been in the Senate for a very short while, Oren still felt the need to prove himself. For two previous confirmation hearings, Mina remembered how much information he had collected and consistently sifted through. As a public servant, Oren felt it was his duty to ensure the protection of the people.

"I'm here for the people," Oren used to say. "That's why they elected me. Not only are they my people, we are one people."

Mina remembered his words endearingly.

Oren went above and a little beyond what was expected in his background checks. He had always been that way and Mina found his commitment inspiring. In her profession, she dealt with finances and policies without much opportunity to be a champion to the people. She used to tell Oren that she was jealous of him.

"Jealous of me, baby? Why?" he'd ask.

"Ahhh, because you have a heart for folks you don't know and who sometimes don't give a damn about you. I'm not like that. I don't have that."

Oren would smile and hold her close.

"You're right. I do. And perhaps they do not. But it's not about them. I do it for me. And you, my love, are more than you even know."

Mina looked through the file folder on Oren's laptop labeled *RESEARCH*. It confirmed that Oren was working on what he considered his "due diligence." The file called *BACKGROUND* had copies of articles and some medical files—all on Attorney Ibra Marcus.

Mina read the first article carefully. It was the city newspaper in the sports section dated twenty-five years ago.

MARCUS TO CLINCH CHAMPIONSHIP TITLE FOR WASHINGTON PREP HIGH.

Even Mina knew about Washington Prep. It was an elite boarding school in the northeast corridor of the state. Most kids were qualified to get in, and if they did, their parents couldn't afford it. Sending your child to Washington Prep for some was a choice between this elite high school or a middle-of-the-road college. Because of their selectivity, they tended to have a subpar sports program. The fact that they won titles this year was a big deal.

Here they had all-star Ibra Marcus putting them on the map. The picture that accompanied the article was one of a tall, husky teenager, arm in arm with another young man.

There were more articles highlighting Ibra as a phenomenon on the basketball court.

Steven Lakos, point guard, stood beside him in most of the pictures. They seemed to have been a pair to be reckoned with.

Mina perused the articles and came to student files from Washington Prep. She found detailed accounts of disciplinary actions taken against Ibra in his four years at Washington Prep. There were at least seven allegations of sexual misconduct with fellow students and two with students at a neighboring school. Young women gave statements of instances when Ibra said highly sexual and very inappropriate things. Four young women reported being fondled and cornered by Ibra. One young girl said that Ibra chased her down the hall and forced her into the boys' bathroom. According to her report, he pinned her to the wall and ripped her shirt off. The only reason she was able to escape was because another boy entered the bathroom. The reports were initiated by the dean of discipline and were copied to the headmaster of the school. Mina checked and re-checked thoroughly, but there seemed to have been no follow-up or actions taken as a result of these reports.

Following those written allegations were four additional allegations of assault and breach of peace. Reading further, Mina expected that it would have named fellow teammates or rival teammates, considering how seriously Ibra took the game. She was flabbergasted to read the names of four other young women who reported varying degrees of physical assault at the hands of Ibra. One reported that he punched her in her back repeatedly and shoved her into a wall. She suffered minor injuries from the incident but was treated and released from the school infirmary.

Again, Mina marveled at how there were no disciplinary actions taken against him. She even checked his attendance record. Stellar. He never missed a day of school and was never suspended.

Ibra ended up receiving glowing recommendations for his college applications from the dean of academics, dean of discipline, and the headmaster.

After reading through the college transcripts and reports, Mina found striking similarities. In college, Ibra was consistently on the dean's list, freshman year through senior year. He was very gifted and it came through clearly. He was on the cusp of genius status. His senior thesis was chosen to be shared at the national convention for political science and prelaw aspirants. He wrote articles for the campus paper, letters to the editor, as well as op-ed pieces nearly monthly. That was coupled with the fact that he was still making quite a name for himself as a basketball player. On the court, he was the freshman high scorer and received numerous accolades for his game-winning plays. He was chosen to be the scholar athlete of the year for two years—his sophomore and junior years. From the looks of it, Ibra Marcus had been a hard worker for many years.

Although she had found out about the disgraceful high school incidents, Mina didn't find anything in his college transcripts. His record was stellar and seemingly squeaky clean. She stood up and stretched, realizing that a few hours had passed since she'd entered Oren's office. She glanced around the room and was comforted by what she saw on the bookshelf and the wall and the side tables. They were all mementos of them—their life together. She welled up with tears as she considered the void deep inside. Her heart raced a bit and she started to feel a little faint. She felt pressure on her chest, which scared her. The pressure turned into soothing and she began to relax again. Breathing in, she caught the light scent of sandalwood. She loved it so much.

Unsure of whether she would ever feel up to entering Oren's office again, Mina decided to sit back down and gather a better understanding of the secrets her husband kept. She continued reading the mass of documents filed under *I. Marcus—records*.

She pulled up a series of complaints that were initiated against Ibra when he was a college student. Her eyes opened wide as saucers when she read the charges and allegations.

"Two counts of assault and battery. Three no, four counts of assault with a deadly weapon," Mina read out loud and shook her head. "Who does this? Who is this man?"

She continued reading. "Multiple counts of sexual misconduct." She leafed through the rest of the document quickly. A few words jumped out at her. Rape and coercion. It seemed that Ibra Marcus had a very extensive criminal record. The vast majority of these allegations were violent. However, upon further investigation, Mina learned that Ibra was never prosecuted for even one of these allegations. After being filed, the complaints were nulled. They virtually did not exist beyond the piece of paper or the virtual paper that they now remained on.

Mina took a minute to collect her thoughts. They were wild and rampant. She could only imagine, if she, an outsider, was feeling confused and disgusted, how did Oren feel after he discovered this? There is no way he kept it to himself. She knew Oren Blake and he'd never stand for this silently.

She massaged her temples and sat up again, eyes fixated on the screen. Recorded separately from the complaints and allegations, Mina found a series of affidavits. All were from women. One woman, Tanya, attested to events at the local bar with Ibra and his teammates.

She wrote:

We met at the bar that night. They were just coming off a huge win earlier and the whole bar was celebrating with them. All these guys were buying him and his friends drinks. They were getting sloshed and we were all having a good time. My girlfriends and I were out just for the fun of it. My girlfriend was dating one of the basketball players. She said they liked to party and I had just broken up with my boyfriend and I needed a distraction. Well, I found one all right. From the moment we were introduced, he was all over me. He was moving fast, considering I didn't know him from Adam. But my girls were like I should just go with it. I let him get all touchy-feely. I was into it at first. Then he started to take it too far. He tried to really touch me, like sexually. Right there in the bar in front of his friends. I pushed his hand away and pried the other off me. I was uncomfortable and embarrassed. He ignored my protests and kept at it. He'd grab at me and say, "Hey, Steve, check this out," and try to fondle me again. The more his friend Steve laughed, the more Ibra would try something. I realized that I was a pawn for them to get their jollies.

Mina was starting to get a good picture of this man. She saw a few more affidavits and read them all. Another woman, Sandra, had a startling account.

She wrote:

Ibra and I knew each other from around campus. We'd see each other from time to time because we had classes in the same building. He was nice and very handsome. He asked me out for drinks after midterms. I thought, why not? We met off campus at a small local bar. When we walked in, the bartenders and a few of the waitresses knew him by name. They really catered to us and treated me like royalty. I absolutely loved it. He was a bit aggressive though and I should have seen it coming. He ordered my drink for me although we had never been out before. Again, I thought nothing of it because all in all, I was having a great time. When my drink came, it was a bit too strong. He forced me to drink it saying that I was wasting his money and did I know how many other girls would kill to be where I was that night? I felt awful but drank it. He had the bartender keep them coming. I

must have had three before I really started feeling like
crap. The thing is, I don't remember him drinking much.
But truthfully, I don't remember much about that night.
It's all patchy after that. I know I started feeling woozy
and told him I was ready to go. At some point, I found
myself in his back seat laid out without my shirt or bra.
He was in the front seat with some guy I didn't know. I
remember asking for my clothes and he slapped me across
the face. Hard too. The rest I don't remember. But my
roommate told me that he and some other guy dropped me
off at my room. At least they had the decency to put my
shirt back on. I don't know what happened or who it
happened with. My roommate encouraged me to go to the
university infirmary the next day. The nurse practitioner
did a rape kit and found traces of semen. I didn't have sex
with that man—or any man. Not that I know of. It's all
so confusing. I just don't know anymore.

Mina was done with this Ibra guy. Whatever he was into was regularly dismissed by school authorities. Nothing stuck on him. Even the nature of the affidavits was painted in a way that made the women sound loony. Mina could just imagine how demonized these poor young women would be if they came out with these stories.

"Abuse at the hands of star student-player-athlete, Ibra Marcus?" Mina mused. "I'm sure no one took you ladies seriously." Sighing deeply,

Mina felt entranced. She wanted to learn as much as she could about Ibra Marcus.

✠

CHAPTER 15: INJURY STRIKES

Mina was focused with laser-like attention on the unfolding story of Ibra Marcus. She had uncovered his propensity to take charge and his natural leader abilities. Academically he was gifted and athletically he was exceptionally talented. He also had a way with women and a particularly aggressive way of taking charge with them throughout his high school and college careers. Mina sifted through article after article indicating the college lauded him for his talent on the court. She expected to see his name among those who were going to declare and go pro in his junior year of college. With all of the accounts of his talent, she was sure he would have elected to play professional ball.

A video news clip and follow-up article clarified things for her in no time. The sports anchor spoke:

TRAGEDY HAS HIT OUR BASKETBALL COMMUNITY. STAR CENTER, IBRA MARCUS HAS INDEED SUFFERED A CAREER-ENDING INJURY. DOCTORS HAVE CONFIRMED THAT HIS TORN ACL WILL REQUIRE ANOTHER ROUND OF SURGERY AND THIS IS THE END OF HIS PROMISING BASKETBALL CAREER.

Pictures flooded the newscast of students and basketball players from all over holding up *GET WELL IBRA* signs. There were many tears as students and staff bawled when Ibra's athletic career ended.

Mina felt a temporary pang of sadness for the man she was getting to know.

And that was the end of his career. She found nothing more on how he coped with it. "If history was any indication," she mused, "Ibra probably got wasted, assaulted some women, and started some fights."

The next prominently labeled file folder was *I. Marcus-Postgrad.*

Without even thinking about the stories that would be revealed here, Mina dug in yet again. Oblivious to thirst or hunger, she sat in Oren's chair and immersed herself, the way Oren would have. She was starting to get a better picture of why Oren was so relentless in his pursuit of truth. But he was like that with everything; he pushed for transparency and accountability from all he touched.

Now, even in his death, Mina felt so close to him. She knew Oren was a part of her. She thought about whether he was the one pushing her to put the pieces together. Perhaps this could be her contribution to the world that Oren was so passionate about. Mina knew Oren loved her with all his heart and soul; she loved him enough to keep going.

"But how? How did you put your hands on this, babe?" She looked to the ceiling and searched it, desperate for the answer.

Mina continued to read and became even more scared for her husband. She was certain that this information was privileged and there was no way Oren should have been able to access this; nor should she have been able to.

In the *POSTGRAD* file, Mina found the expected. Ibra was accepted to the top law school in the nation. He was offered a full ride to study there. Her mind was blown. "Ibra Marcus. Star athlete. Local boy—did good." In law school, he was the editor of the law review and a member of the Moot Court Team. As was his tendency, Ibra's team made it to the finals every single time. He was not shy about patting himself on the back or singing his own praises. The file even had a portfolio of his finer works: articles, briefs, and memorandums on a variety of topics. He had even entered a few into writing contests and had won. Ibra Marcus was making himself out to be a beast in the legal arena. After reading about how great he was in law school, Mina immediately looked for the affidavits or allegations or complaints lodged against him from unsuspecting women he had abused. She flipped through each document in the file but found nothing. She looked again. There was no way this leopard had changed his spots. Again, she found nothing.

Slightly disappointed at the thought of his complete rehabilitation, she read more of his accomplishments and summer clerkships. This man had the Midas touch and everything he touched turned to gold from Mina's vantage point. He was on his way to the very top, and it was no surprise that now, a few years later, he was up for the attorney general of their fair state.

In an unnamed file on Oren's drive, there were blurbs about the best and brightest in pro basketball. Steven Lakos was the number eight draft pick the same year Ibra tore his ACL. There were a handful of articles and pictures celebrating Steven. Of course, seated right beside him on draft day was Ibra Marcus. Mina watched the attached video footage and was transfixed by the emotion all over Ibra's face when the announcer called Steve's name. Steve jumped up and hugged Ibra, followed by folks who were likely his parents. As the camera panned on his face, Ibra was caught screaming "Yes! Yes!" He then clapped thunderously with his huge hands.

Mina ran through all the files Oren had created regarding Ibra Marcus. Ibra moved on successfully through law and on to the district attorney's office. The rest of his career was chronicled in the media because Ibra Marcus became known as the DA no one wanted to go up against. He must have brought his competitive nature from the basketball court to the court of law.

The sound of the front door closing and footsteps coming close to the now-closed office door interrupted her thoughts. The steps stopped at the door then retreated from it. Mina heard the steps going upstairs and the guest bedroom door close. She knew she needed to talk to Candace but she couldn't. Not right now.

"What does all this mean? Who is this guy, babe? What were you searching for?" Mina again searched the ceiling for answers but received none.

She went over the files on the flash drive and read them again: starting from Washington Prep and ending at Ibra Marcus's appointment to the DA's office.

✠✠
CHAPTER 16: DETECTIVE TOURE

The sun shone beautifully through the cracks of the blinds in Oren's office. Mina stretched and massaged her shoulder. She rubbed her eyes and rolled her neck back and forth. She wasn't sure what time it was or how long she had been at it. Carefully, she closed the laptop and removed the flash drive. She returned it to the beautiful ornate wooden box. Holding both the key and the box carefully, she headed to her room. The bedroom smelled like mint: a combination of peppermint and spearmint.

Mina found a necklace that Oren had given her but she seldom wore. It was plain but perfect for the key that Mina hung on it before fixing the chain around her neck.

Once downstairs, Mina saw Candace seated at the breakfast table looking troubled.

"Candy, I know we have to talk."

Candace had a faraway look in her eyes.

"Yeah, Mina. We do. What…what…what happened that night?" Candace asked, bewildered.

"I really don't know, Candy," Mina began. "But whatever it was, was real."

"Oh, I know. Just look at your hair."

Mina had almost forgotten. It had been a whole day and she was already used to it. Her lovely thick locks draped her neck.

"Tell you what. I have a few errands to run this morning. How about we have a late lunch together. Meet you right back here at two?"

Candace still looked stressed.

"Okay. Because I have some things to share with you too," she muttered.

Mina walked over to her best friend and gave her a big hug.

"Candy, you've been my rock these past few weeks. There's no way I would have made it without you."

Candace hugged her and seemed hesitant to her let go.

"See you at two."

"Mina, I'm scared for you."

"Don't be," Mina said smiling. "It'll all be just fine."

In the car, she pulled out her phone.

"Detective Toure? I'm on my way now."

***

Detective Toure and Mina sat in the same booth where they'd met just a few days ago. They exchanged pleasantries and both sat quietly for a while.

Detective Toure broke the silence. "You look...different. But nice."

Mina blushed. "Thanks. Have you made any headway?"

"Well, that's some of what I wanted to discuss with you, Mrs. Blake. My supervisor took me off the case. It's now being handled by the chief of police-elect."

"What? Why?" Mina shrieked.

"Shhh." Detective Toure motioned for her to be quiet.

"I really don't know. After it was determined that this is a homicide, the chief-elect told me personally that he'd be handling it, which is kinda crazy, because he has been inundated with work on the rash of recent missing persons cases."

"Oh my God. Is he going to connect with me? Does he know to call me?" Color had drained from her face as she spoke.

"I wouldn't bank on it. He's not known for being a high-touch kind of guy. You'll get information, though. It'll likely just be at a much slower rate."

"You must be freaking kidding me!" Mina yelled.

Detective Toure placed his hand on hers. "Mrs. Blake, please." His eyes pleaded with hers.

Mina looked at his hand and quickly pulled hers from underneath his.

"Okay," Detective Toure said, "tell you what. How about we take a different angle with this?"

Mina looked up to stare at him. She was saddened. "Tell me what you mean," she said almost inaudibly.

"I don't know how good you are at being discreet, but I'd like to suggest that we form an alliance. Your husband's case is obviously big enough to garner the attention of the deputy chief of police, so there must be something to that. And figuring that he was your husband, you probably knew him better than anyone. You must know things."

Mina perked up enough to smile. "An alliance! By that do you mean that we share information with each other in the furtherance of this case?" She clapped her hands as she spoke.

"That's *exactly* what I mean," Detective Toure said. "For some reason, I want to do this for you. This could really jeopardize my job but I'm compelled. Truthfully, I trust you and I have no idea why."

"I'm trustworthy, Detective." She relaxed her shoulders and folded her hands stately on the booth surface. "So, since we're allies, I have something to discuss with you. What do you know about Ibra Marcus?"

Detective Toure scrunched his eyebrows together and cocked his head to the side.

"District Attorney Marcus? He's no nonsense and I'm surprised that you don't know about him. His reputation precedes him."

"Yeah, I know all about his reputation," Mina said sarcastically.

"Huh?" Detective Toure appeared confused. "He's a great guy. An absolute beast in court, but he's a real likable guy. I've met him quite a few times."

"You have? Would you consider him a friend of yours?" Mina asked.

"No, not a friend per se. But we've connected a few times socially with other people. He's in line to be confirmed by the Senate any minute now. He'll probably assume his position in the AG's office in a month."

Detective Toure proceeded to have a love fest recalling Ibra Marcus's recent crackdown on prosecuting crime.

"Attorney Marcus could have written his ticket and gone anywhere, but he chose to come back home. Did you know he grew up right here? He had so many offers from huge law firms around the country. Trial work, defense work, you name it. But again, he chose to come back home and do great work right here. There's a serial rapist out there too and Attorney Marcus was in the midst of the case when this potential appointment came up."

He looked at Mina curiously. "Why do you ask, anyway? What's your interest in him?" Detective Toure had spoken in such glowing terms that Mina hesitated to answer. He continued speaking.

"So the thing about Attorney Ibra is that he is a genius. He has positioned himself perfectly to advance in his career. When his boss the chief district attorney died, he was promoted instantly. It was questionable initially because he was promoted over the deputy state's attorney."

"Wait. The chief died and *he* was promoted over some other attorney? Isn't the deputy attorney the second in command?" Mina asked. She was awestruck. "How is that okay? Sorry to hear that the chief guy died." Mina bowed her head, closed her eyes and made the sign of the cross.

"Yeah, under normal circumstances the deputy state's attorney would be poised to assume the position," the detective began.

"Let me guess. These were not normal circumstances." Mina rolled her eyes.

"Now that I think about it, I guess not. Chief wasn't sick or anything," the detective responded. "It was actually quite tragic and slightly suspicious." Detective Toure's voice trailed off. "He was said to have died from asphyxiation," he continued.

"What! You mean he was strangled?" Mina raised her voice again. "Oh my God. Death plagues you guys here."

"No, no, Mrs. Blake. Not that type of asphyxiation. It was more like anaphylactic shock. He had a severe allergic reaction to shellfish and died before the ambulance and EMT were able to save him. They said he ate a batch of shrimp."

Mina continued looking at the detective incredulously. "Are you serious?" Didn't he know he was allergic to shellfish? Why would he have eaten that?" Shaking her head, Mina pondered the circumstances carefully. "Nevertheless," she continued, "how'd Attorney Marcus get promoted?"

"After the chief DA's unfortunate death, the deputy came down with a debilitating illness. He was prevented from carrying out his job to its fullest extent. He basically became incapacitated, and Attorney Marcus received an instant promotion."

Mina's mouth opened wide. She could not believe what she was hearing. "Doesn't it concern you the way tragedy and death seem to follow him?"

Detective Toure must not have heard her or chose not to respond.

"Detective," she began again, "he's bad news. Trust me. I'm sure of it."

"Mrs. Blake, you're mistaken. He's done a lot for this city. When he was appointed chief state's attorney, he systematically began real efforts to clean this city up. His conviction rates were up, and repeat offenders plummeted because he made sure to throw the book at them."

It was clear to Mina that Attorney Marcus had everyone fooled.

✠✠

CHAPTER 17: LUNCH

Mina's mind was clouded from the moment she left Detective Toure to the moment she saw her friend sitting in the living room waiting for her.

"Hey, lady," Mina said meekly. "Are you okay?"

"I made us lunch." Candace pointed to the side table where Mina's plate sat. It was a lovely garden salad with grilled chicken breast topping it. "You haven't been eating. That won't work, sweetie. Here's your fork."

Mina smiled genuinely and plopped down beside her friend. She took the fork and ate voraciously.

"I'll start," said Candace. "Remember when you asked me about the Orisha and how I responded?"

"Umm hmm," Mina said in between bites.

"It turns out there's a lot we don't know, Mina. I told you about Granny, right? And how she loved Eshu. How he was her favorite. How she had an altar in the house. I told you, right?"

This time, Mina just shook her head.

"Well, what I didn't tell you was that Granny was a priestess. She always said that I'd come to love and honor the Orisha. One day I'd accept it. She'd tell me that as Yoruba people that is what I must believe. But that was Grandma, and it was different in my house. Mama always drilled Christianity. I don't think I ever told you, but the missionaries came to Mama's village when she was just a small child. They offered Christianity and it caused a real split in the village. Mama accepted it and ended up going to live with a minister in the village who was also a Christian. That's Baba's father. I guess that's why Mama and Baba got married. They were like the only Christians in the village. Everyone else was Ifa."

Mina put her fork down and reached for Candace's arm to give it a squeeze. "There's no shame in your heritage, Candy. We have an illustrious history and we should be proud of our people."

"I mean, I'm proud, Mina. But I never thought the Orisha gods were anything more than tradition that the old folks held on to. Seeing what happened the other night, I realized that something was happening."

Mina stared at her plate. Twirling a spinach leaf with her fork, she was so fixated it was like she was talking to the leaves. "You saw all that right? You saw what he…he…you saw what happened didn't you? Tell me I'm not crazy!"

"If I hadn't seen it with my own eyes, I wouldn't believe it. But no, sweetie. You're not crazy. Not in the least," Candy responded.

They recounted the antics that they witnessed. Mina chatted incessantly, taking true advantage of the outlet.

"Mina, you were powerless. Powerless against him," Candace said.

"You don't understand. Once I let go, I was so powerful, Candy," she tried to explain.

"But you couldn't even control your own body! And your body...so many changes." Candace fondled her hair as they spoke.

Mina relaxed enough to share her true feelings about whom or what she was experiencing. "Do you think it's Oren, in spirit form?" she asked.

"I really don't know, Mina. I guess it could be. I was taught that our spirits are energy and energy can't end. It just transfers. I guess the Oren energy could be what you feel so strongly."

"But what about this Eshu character? I don't know anything about him. Why would he have sought me out? I mean, if it is him and all. The energy that inhabits me, speaks to me. Calls me Queen."

Candace turned as white as the blinds. For a beautifully dark woman, she became quite pale. "You

didn't tell me that part. He calls you Queen?"
Candace asked.

She turned away and fumbled in her pocket for
her phone. She yanked it up and dialed a number.

"Hello, Aunty. This is Candace. Do you have a
moment?"

Candace spoke with her aunt for a good while.
Sure that Candace had a purpose for calling out of the
blue, the conversation turned very quickly. She told
her aunt of the night visits thus far. She responded
with a few guttural "Uh huhs" and "Mmmm. All
right."

After speaking for ten to fifteen minutes,
Candace agreed to call her aunt back tomorrow.

"So? What happened? What'd she say? Why'd
you even call?" Mina peppered her friend with
questions.

"Aunty told me something that I'd heard from
Granny when I was a child. She said that the Orisha
are here for us to grow. When you think about it,
there are elements of them everywhere in creation.
Each Orisha or trait is a way of identifying our
creation and existence and this is how we thank our
Creator for it. But Granny always told us that if the
Orisha came to you out of the blue, there was a
purpose. Sometimes it would be to point you back to
you. In other words, sometimes it was to figure out if

you've been here before and to continue on with your purpose."

"If I've been here before? Do you mean like reincarnation?" Mina asked, her eyes wild.

"Yeah, sweetie, that's exactly what I mean. I mean for example, what's your name?"

"Candy, you know my name. Mina. Remember me?" she asked playfully.

"Your whole given name is Aminatu Cisse."

"Yeah. And?"

"Really, Mina? Do you not know who you are? Not even your name?"

"No, of course I know that. I was named after Aminatu, the warrior of many centuries ago in Zaria."

"Did it ever occur to you that you might have been more than named?"

"What? No, Candy…My mom named me because she said I have a warrior spirit. She said giving birth to me was like the fight of her life. Hers and mine, as a matter of fact."

Candace chuckled. "I'm not surprised. But Mina, the warrior Aminatu is more than a mere woman talented in military combat. She was royalty, regal, majestic."

Mina gave Candace the serious deep side eye.

Candace stood and paced the room, determined to prove her case.

"You're not buying it, huh? Let's recap. So the Orisha manifest in your house. Eshu inhabits your body and changes things in there around. You transform, right before my eyes, but you can't comprehend the centuries' old philosophy of reincarnation? Really…"

Mina was not prepared to accept these temporary changes in her life as something more permanent or long lasting. Although inconceivable, she thought that at any moment, it would all go away.

"Okay, Mina. I can't believe I'm saying this but just sit with that for a few days. You ever consider that idea that Eshu came to you to point you to the truth? Your true being? The essence of you that was here before and the fact that there's work to do now?"

Mina resumed eating quietly as she pondered her friend's words.

✠ CHAPTER 18: THE GYM

"Are we still allies, Mrs. Blake? I haven't heard from you in days," Detective Toure asked playfully over the phone.

"I've had a lot on my mind," Mina said. "Glad you called. Still allies, though. Although it seems that the assignment has stalled. Do you have any information for me especially since you're officially off the case?"

"The department has been reeling. Another woman has gone missing. We have an outright rash of missing persons right now, so no, I don't have new information."

"Missing persons, huh?"

"Missing *women* only. Be careful out there, Mrs. Blake."

"Oh, I will, Detective. I recently took up kickboxing and I realize I have quite an aptitude for fighting." She let out a laugh.

"Is that right? Maybe you should come to my gym tonight down on Grand Street. 1200. They're having an open house and MMA demonstration," Detective Toure said.

"MMA?" Mina asked

"Oh yeah. Mixed Martial Arts. I'm sure you'd love it. Especially if you're really getting into kickboxing. That's how the gym drums up business. Give away a lesson or two and hope that you come back for more."

"Huh. Maybe I will," she said. "Okay, Detective, so tell me about these women."

"Not much to tell in that department either, unfortunately. All between the ages of twenty-eight and forty-one. Their looks are a range. Mixed races and features are just as mixed. All I can tell you is that they are pretty women and highly educated."

"By highly, what do you mean? College graduates?"

"Oh no, Mrs. Blake. I mean college professors, surgeons, and attorneys."

"Get outta here! No way! What's going on? How many women?"

"Five so far. God willing there are no more. I'm telling you, this is the A-one priority in the department. Not that the other things aren't being attended to, but these women might still be alive is all."

"I understand. If that was my sister or best friend or aunt or cousin out there, I'd want you guys pooling all your efforts for her."

"Speaking of which, I've been meaning to ask you. Do you have a sister?" His voice trembled a bit at the end.

Not sure whether to take him seriously, Mina laughed.

"I mean th…that we're allies and I don't know anything about you," Detective Toure offered meekly.

"I'm an open book," she said. "My parents immigrated to the United States from Nigeria when I was a small child. It's only me. I had a brother, but he was killed by a stray bullet in conflict. So my parents and I left Nigeria and I've been right here ever since."

"Oh, your parents are local then?"

"No, both have since passed. It was just me. Then me and Oren. So yeah. It's just me."

Detective Toure became quiet and neither of them said anything for a short while.

"Will I see you tonight?" the detective asked.

"At the MMA demo? You probably will," Mina said before hanging up.

***

Mina wore a spandex outfit that hugged and held all her thickness together. She walked into the building as though she were expected—with a great air of confidence. She weaved in and out of the gathering crowd with ease. Candace trailed a little farther back and tugged on her booty shorts a few times. Mina was uncomfortably cognizant of how her own curves were exploited in her outfit.

"Can we all gather to the center?" a short very buff man with a surprisingly high voice said loudly.

"C'mon people. Get up in here. Gather around." He sighed and waved at the air a few times.

"It is my honor and privilege to present the MMA style of Kimber Whyte. Please welcome her!"

The crowd obediently clapped but was in no way as enthusiastic as the man.

A tall, slender woman approached the center of the human circle. She was gorgeous and ripped. Muscle definition was everywhere and her abs looked chiseled. Her hair was braided back neatly in two. Mina couldn't help but compare herself to Kimber Whyte and she was exceptionally jealous. As Kimber spoke, Mina hung on her every word.

"Okay, everybody. Listen up. My name is Kimber Whyte and I'm the middleweight reigning champion. I'm going to teach you some of my signature moves as well as a few of the most effective self-defense moves. How does that sound?"

The crowd again applauded. Mina clapped her hands loudly, smiling the entire time.

Kimber demonstrated some of her finest MMA combinations. She punched and kicked the air showing how beautiful her form was. Deliberate yet graceful, Kimber was a marvel both physically and athletically. Mina couldn't get over her physique. Distracted and painting her own picture of having the body of her dreams, Mina didn't hear the question. Her eyes were cast upward when she felt a firm hand on her shoulder.

"How about you? You down for an up close and personal lesson?"

Mina caught Kimber's eyes and realized she couldn't weasel her way out of it.

"Sure. Why not," Mina said flippantly, shrugging her shoulders.

"Here we go. Don't worry, honey. You won't get hurt...much," Kimber whispered winking.

Kimber launched a slow and calculated jab to Mina's chest. Stepping aside, she looked surprised when the jab did not connect.

"Mmm." Kimber's eyes twinkled. "Okay."

Kimber initiated a faster kick that was intended to lightly tap Mina's sternum. Mina leaned back and went into a quick backflip. After Mina landed on her feet, Kimber tried another jab. Mina did a split, again avoiding the connection.

"Whoa!" the crowd cheered nearly in unison.

Kimber grinned. "You're not a novice, huh?"

Wide-eyed, Mina shrugged her shoulders in utter confusion and stood up.

"Want to spar for five minutes? Give our attendees an impromptu show?"

"Five minutes, though. Cause really, that's all I got left," Mina said, bending over.

The crowd erupted into laughter and the friendly competition was on.

Kimber took it easy on Mina but still seemed to employ effort. A roundhouse kick moved the air above Mina's head. Hit by an immediate adrenaline rush, Mina moved effortlessly into perfect Capoeira formation. Back and forth, Kimber and Mina orchestrated a fighter's dance. Kick for kick. Punch for flip. Kimber slid her foot out to trip Mina but instead, Mina moved into a backflip followed by a crouch and sprang into the air with an explosive kick. The timer blared and the two opponents stopped.

"Miss Kimber Whyte, everybody!" The gym manager held Kimber's hand high in the air.

"What's your name, ma'am?"

"A-mi-na-tu," Mina said slowly.

"And Miss Aminatu!" The manager patted Mina forcefully on the back. "Nice job! Nice job!" he said, gushing.

"For tonight only, you can get a group instruction session with Miss Kimber if you sign up at the front desk in the next five minutes."

A group of nearly fifteen folks rushed the front desk. Kimber approached Mina.

"That was impressive. Aminatu is it?"

"Yeah. Thanks."

"I expected that tonight was going to be boring. I'm used to having a few guys ogle my body and challenge me to arm wrestling or something. Then there are the chicks who stare in my face but are seriously checking me out." She rolled her eyes and placed a hand on her hips. "But instead, this was a blast! Where'd you learn that Capoeira style? My trainer did Capoeira. That's old-school style. Nice."

"I really don't know. It must be in the blood somewhere..." Mina's voice trailed off.

Kimber grabbed Mina lightly by the arm.

"How about this," Kimber said, giddy. "Come by the gym on a Tuesday night. My trainer would love to see this."

"Kimber!" The gym manager waved her over.

"Gotta run. See you at the gym." Kimber winked at Mina and took off in the direction of the manager and an impatient group of wannabes.

Mina let her locks down and shook them back and forth. The row of gym TVs blared the same sitcom. Canned laughter drowned out any attempts at conversation.

"What'd I miss?" Detective Toure spoke loudly from behind her.

Candace inched in close to where Mina and the detective stood.

"You missed this woman demonstrating Capoeira perfectly." Candace thumbed in Mina's direction.

"Detective Scott Toure, this is my best friend, Candace."

"Oh, so *this* is Candace? A pleasure."

The two shook hands as Mina kept on talking. "I wouldn't say all that, Candy. I've seen Capoeira before and this was not perfect. Didn't look like what the guy on TV does."

"Seen Capoeira, Mrs. Blake? Don't you study the form?"

"No, not exactly. But it was an exhilarating experience, to say the least. My body took over and just knew exactly what to do."

The detective looked from one face to the other.

"I'm missing something, aren't I?" he asked.

Candace was about to speak when they heard:

"WE INTERRUPT THIS REGULARLY SCHEDULED PROGRAM TO BRING YOU A NEWS BRIEF LIVE FROM DOWNTOWN."

All of the TVs now featured an enthusiastic reporter.

"ON THE HEELS OF THE REPORT OF ANOTHER MISSING WOMAN, OUR CHIEF OF POLICE HAS CALLED A PRESS CONFERENCE."

"Another missing woman?" Mina turned to face Detective Toure. His eyes bulged and he adjusted his horn-rimmed glasses.

The cameras panned to the podium. A large older man decked in regalia stood in the center, flocked by a host of men and women in uniform.

LIVE FROM THE PRECINCT was displayed across the base of the screen.

"THANK YOU FOR GATHERING TONIGHT. IN LIGHT OF OUR RECENT RASH OF MISSING PERSONS NOT ONLY HERE IN OUR CITY BUT UNFORTUNATELY ELSEWHERE IN THE STATE, THE DEPARTMENT NOW REGARDS THIS AS A STATE OF EMERGENCY AND OUR RESPONSE IS IMMEDIATE. I'VE BEEN IN CONSTANT COMMUNICATION WITH THE

GOVERNOR AND HE SUPPORTS THIS AS OUR
DEPARTMENT'S PRIORITY. WE ARE CONCERNED FOR THE
CITIZENS OF OUR FAIR CITY, AND YOUR HEALTH AND
SAFETY ARE PARAMOUNT! OUR COMMITMENT IS TO YOU
AND BRINGING OUR MISSING HOME. WE WILL NOT
TOLERATE AN ATTACK ON OUR CITIZENS! I'LL BE HEADING
THIS OPERATION PERSONALLY AND WILL BE ASSISTED BY
THE DEPUTY CHIEF OF POLICE, MY SON, STEVEN LAKOS."

Mina's mouth dropped. She grabbed Detective Toure's arm and shook it violently.

"Lakos! Steven Lakos is the chief of police?" she asked.

"No, that's Robert Lakos," Detective Toure said as he peeled Mina's tight grip from his forearm. "Steven is his son. Is this news to you?"

Deputy Police Chief Lakos took the podium. He was about six four and slender. Even through his uniform, it was evident that he was very fit.

"GOOD EVENING. NOT ONLY ARE THERE MISSING
PERSONS, BUT WE HAVE RECEIVED REPORTS OF A SERIAL
RAPIST ATTACKING UNSUSPECTING WOMEN IN OUR CITY
AND IN NEIGHBORING CITIES. WE'RE ASKING ALL CITY
RESIDENTS, NOT ONLY WOMEN, TO BE ON THE LOOKOUT
FOR A MAN REPORTEDLY WEARING A BLACK MASK AND
BLUE TRENCH COAT. HE IS SAID TO BE AGGRESSIVE AND
DANGEROUS. PLEASE DO NOT TAKE THIS LIGHTLY AND
CONTACT THE PRECINCT WITH ANY SIGHTINGS."

"Detective, we have to talk," Mina said insistently.

✠✠
CHAPTER 19: BELIEVE ME

Mina put the kettle on and Candace fluttered about the kitchen making a boxed quick bread. Detective Toure sat at the table and listened as Mina spoke.

She told him of Oren's research, careful to omit how she was driven to it. Mina painstakingly recounted the files, articles, and records that Oren had compiled. She shared anecdotes of how thorough Oren was in everything and his duty as senator compelled him to do that, and more.

Detective Toure tapped nervously on the counter during Mina's entire explanation.

"I know this is far-fetched and I know how much you respect Ibra Marcus—but, he's not the man you think he is. Want to see the actual documents?"

"Candy, can we borrow your laptop?"

She nodded. Candy had remained in the kitchen the whole time. First, as she'd already told Mina privately, there was no way she would let her best friend be alone with some man. Nope. Never. And second, she seemed eager to hear the entire story as well.

Mina ran upstairs to her room and pulled the ornate wooden box from her closet. Producing the key from around her neck, she unlocked the box and withdrew the flash drive. She felt a wave surround her; it felt like a warm hug had entered her soul. She paused from rushing back downstairs to enjoy the wave of energy that invaded her. She stretched out her arms and swayed for a little. She breathed it all in and returned downstairs.

"All right, here it is," she mumbled as she inserted the flash drive.

"Mmmm. You just put on a new scent, Mrs. Blake?" Detective Toure started sniffing the air. "I know that scent. It's so earthy. What's it called again?"

"Banana bread is ready," Candace interrupted with setups in hand.

Mina loaded the file display for Detective Toure. Candace sat down beside him to read as well. After about an hour, he pushed the laptop away.

"I think I've seen enough for today. I can't believe I'm saying this, Mrs. Blake, but Attorney Marcus is definitely not the man I thought he was."

Mina exhaled, relieved.

"I'm not sure how much your husband knew or what else he discovered. But this may be why he was targeted."

Detective Toure's hands shook as he fiddled with his glasses.

"You need to find out what was on his work computer, Mrs. Blake. Can you make up a reason to get back to the capitol and into the office space?"

Mina lowered her eyes and hunched her shoulders. "Are you serious, Detective? I don't know if I can."

"I'll go with you, Mina," Candace said.

"Actually, Candace, I was going to propose you have a different role for you."

Candace looked at him with interest. "Oh? What are you proposing?"

The detective cleared his throat and tried to steady his hands. "This is the thing. To get an angle on our priority, which is Oren Blake's murder, we need to approach this from two sides. We need to find out as much as we can about what lead Oren was following. Mrs. Blake, whatever you uncover will implicate someone or someones. Whoever has the most to lose will be our lead. And from the other side, we need to get a pulse on Attorney Marcus. What kind of man are we about to confirm as attorney general?"

"That makes sense to me," Mina said.

"We really sound like a team!" Candace chirped. "What's my role?"

"Ahhh, all right. Now we get to you. Candace, I'd like you to accompany me to the mayor's event tomorrow night. Deputy Chief Lakos and Attorney Marcus will definitely be there. Attorney Marcus is supposed to give an address. If you come with me Candace, then maybe we can get near Attorney Marcus. Sorry, Mrs. Blake, you're too visible to come right now."

"I understand," Mina said, although she was slightly disappointed.

✠✠

CHAPTER 20: MAYOR'S EVENT

Candace was gorgeous and ready for the detective to pick her up. She acted like a schoolgirl getting ready for her first date. She changed her outfit three times and made sure her makeup was impeccable. The result was absolute beauty. Mina had to remind herself that Candace going out with a very handsome man while Mina stayed home was all for the sake of the case. She convinced herself that she wanted a night to herself anyway.

Detective Toure showed up at the door moments later. He had a bouquet of flowers in hand. A mix of carnations, roses, and tulips, Mina's favorites. He promptly handed them to Candace right after they embraced with a hug that, from Mina's perspective, lasted too long.

"Mrs. Blake, very nice to see you." Detective Toure offered his hand. "Any success getting to the capitol?"

"No, I went on to my husband's desktop instead. I was looking for more information. You'll never guess what I found."

"Oooh! Tell me." The detective's eyes sparkled as he spoke.

Mina was pleased that he looked so interested. "I found that Senator Sam Kingsly and Attorney Marcus were classmates in law school. They were on the same trial advocacy team. And they both interned for the same judicial court for two summers. I'm pretty sure that's a conflict for the chair of the committee. But just to be sure, I decided to look up the law school dean. Amazingly enough, he still works for the school and in the same capacity! In any case, he remembered the school's stand-out alums: 'Here at the law school, we are so proud to have such distinguished alums.'" Mina tried to put on her most distinguished voice.

Detective Toure shook his head in agreement and met her eyes as she continued.

"I perhaps may have possibly kinda led the dean to believe that our interview was going to be aired that evening—because of the upcoming confirmation hearing. He sang like a bird!" She grinned. "He remarked to me, unprompted mind you, that Sam and Ibra were as thick as thieves. Sam was a great help and support to Ibra, especially when he missed nearly a month of school. That's when I asked why it had taken so long." She paused for a moment.

"And that is when the dean responded to me like I was completely uninformed about life. 'Don't you remember? Everyone saw when Steven Lakos, star point guard, shattered his knees during the playoffs. You really don't remember that?' he continued to ask me as if I should have known."

Mina continued. "But wait, there's more. Steven and Ibra grew up together like brothers, in the same house practically. When Steven had to have a battery of surgeries so that he could walk again, Ibra took an extended leave from school. He supported Steven and traveled back and forth the whole time. So apparently law school is demanding. The dean described it as 'a jealous mistress,' or something like that." Mina paused. "Ibra missed so much work that when he returned he was in serious academic danger. But all he had to do was pass the final. Now, Sam Kingsly worked with him and brought him up to speed and shared the notes, from what the dean told me. After all that, they became buddies."

Mina looked pleased with herself. "Do you believe that, Detective?"

The detective had focused his complete attention on Mina and her story. Shaking his head, he said, "This is unreal. All these connections staring us right in the face. Do you still want to head up to the capitol? Senator Kingsly might be there. Don't want you running up against something or someone you're not prepared for."

Mina smiled confidently. "No, I got this. I can handle it."

***

The mayor's fundraising event was the local who's who for the state. State officials and local celebrities flocked the downtown hotel to attend. Candace felt quite comfortable; she looked like a celebrity herself.

"This is the plan, Candace," Detective Toure began. "You mix and mingle and see if you can talk it up with either of our guys. I'll text you updates."

"Got it." She smiled, radiantly.

They split up in the ballroom and worked the room. Detective Toure ate hors d'oeuvres and chatted with other city officials. Candace, a naturally social person, had no problem meeting people and making small talk. She held a glass of wine and made her way from one end of the room to the other.

After about an hour, weary of the crowd, she slipped outside. She sat on an outdoor bench and looked at the stars. The air was crisp but the night was lovely. Instinctively she rubbed her bare shoulders as she sat.

"Cold?" a deep, penetrating voice interrupted her stargazing. Candace looked up to find the most gorgeous man she had ever seen standing in front of her.

Shaken from the interruption, she remained silent.

"I'm sorry. Did I startle you? It's just that a beautiful woman such as yourself has no business being out here alone and cold."

Still silent, Candace's heart raced.

"I'm Ibra Marcus. And you are?" he said with an outstretched hand.

"I'm Candace."

"Hello, Candace. It is my absolute pleasure to meet you. You still look cold. Can I offer you my jacket? Or is there someone in your life who wouldn't appreciate that?"

He was sexy and sophisticated. Not at all the repulsive sociopath Mina described. Candace blushed and was instantly coy.

"No, there's no one like that in my life right now."

"May I?" Ibra took off his suit jacket and draped it around her shoulders.

Quickly disinterested in returning to the event inside, Candace allowed Ibra to remain focused solely on her. He stood very close to her. He smelled divine and he must have known it. Candace stood up, prepared to leave.

"No, stay. Please, Candace." His deep velvet voice melted her resolve. She sat back down and continued to enjoy the moment. They talked and laughed in the secluded area outside of the hotel.

After a nearly an hour, Candace heard her phone vibrate.

"Do you have to get that?" Ibra pouted and placed a tender hand on her shoulder.

"Umm…I guess it can wait."

"Wonderful. I'm not prepared to end the most interesting conversation with the most exquisite woman I've ever met."

Candace tried not to be affected by his words and only smiled.

They chatted some more, primarily about Ibra's fascinating work projects and Candace's career.

"You are so enchanting, Candace. I'd love to talk to you more."

Her phone vibrated again. She silenced it.

"How about we get together after this for a late-night cocktail? I have a favorite little spot close by."

Before she knew it, Candace gave Ibra her number and agreed to meet him later on that night.

Her phone vibrated again. A frazzled young man ran up to them.

"Attorney Marcus! I've been looking all over for you. The mayor would like you to address the crowd."

"Welp, I guess that's that, Candace," Ibra said, preparing to leave.

"I guess so," Candace said sweetly.

Ibra helped her to her feet. She handed him back his jacket and he grabbed her hand. Moving his hands to her waist, he slowly pulled her close to him. He whispered in her ear and she felt his warm breath on her neck. "I'll see you later."

He kissed her lightly on the neck, his beard tickling her skin. His lips were soft and perfectly moist. Candace got chills as he pulled away.

Ibra moved swiftly back to the event. Candace lagged behind a little, processing what had happened.

At the door, Detective Toure paced back and forth. "Candace! Where have you been?" he demanded.

"Oh, were you looking for me?" she asked, smiling and acting coy.

He looked annoyed. "I texted you like four times. Never mind. Are you ready to go?"

"We're leaving? Already?" Candace whined.

"Yeah, they're wrapping up now basically anyway."

"Oh, okay." Candace tried to hide her disappointment.

She was unusually silent in the car.

"How'd you make out tonight? Did you meet Marcus or Lakos?"

"Uh…no," Candace said looking out the window. "How about you?"

"I've met Ibra Marcus before. I was trying to cozy up to him tonight, but he was so elusive! Man, every time I went over to where I saw him last, he was gone. I don't think he spoke with any one group or person for longer than six or seven minutes. Not from what I saw, at least."

Candace leaned in as Detective Toure spoke.

"Now, I did see Chief Lakos though. He kept more to himself than I thought. I was sure he would be introducing Steven as his successor during the party. But for whatever reason he was really reserved tonight. Steven was there. He and I are acquaintances, but you can't really say we are friends. We chatted briefly, nothing having to do with work, though. I'm going to have to get inside that man's psyche. I'm formulating a plan. Who did you meet? Anyone interesting?"

"I stayed busy, mostly small talk. I wonder how Mina made out tonight. She probably would have enjoyed this event," Candace spoke still gazing out the window.

"What do you say about grabbing a quick bite to eat? They had tons of hors d'oeuvres but I really didn't eat. I'm a bit peckish." The detective sounded hopeful.

Candace checked her cell phone another time.

"Not tonight. Thanks, though, Detective. I think I'll just go back to Mina." Candace tried to sound upbeat as she spoke.

"Oh okay. No problem. Thanks for coming out with me tonight. I think we'll make good headway over the next few days."

By the time they returned to the house, Candace was itching to leave. The hug good night was nothing like the hug hello. Barely brushing against him, she rushed away from the car and into the house.

✠✠

CHAPTER 21: AT THE BAR

"How was it?" Mina asked.

"Uneventful," Candace replied. "Met a bunch of people, had some good wine, but apart from that nothing much."

Mina remained quiet for a few seconds. "Are you sure?"

Candace started up the stairs to the guest room. "No," she called over her shoulder. "I'm okay."

It was nearly 11:00 p.m. when Candace's phone rang. She picked it up quickly and tried her best not to sound anxious.

"Hello."

"Candace, this is Ibra. You should come down and meet me. I'm at Quincy's on Broad Street. Will you come?" he asked. His velvet voice dripped with appeal.

"Definitely. See you in fifteen minutes!" Candace nearly yelled into the phone, unable to contain her excitement.

She trotted downstairs nonchalantly and headed to the front door.

"Hey, girlie. Where are you running off to? It's kind of late, don't you think?" Mina asked poking her head around the corner and tapping her wrist.

"Oh me? R...r...right now?" Candace stuttered. "Well, um, Detective Toure asked me to meet him for drinks tonight."

Mina stepped into the hallway and folded her arms across her chest. "Oh, he did? Really? That's nice, I guess. You two seem to be really hitting it off. He sure didn't hug me the way he embraced you. Looks to me like there's something more developing."

Candace paused and spoke slowly. "With us? No, I'm just getting to know him. Plus, seems like we are a team right? I should know my teammates. Gotta run. Told him I'd be there in ten minutes."

"Okay, bestie. Have fun. I might be up. Who knows." Mina smiled. "I love you. Be safe."

Candace was already out the door and closing it behind her as Mina spoke.

She took a quick peek around the bar and strutted into Quincy's, spotting Ibra in the corner. He was just as sexy and suave as he was mere hours ago. He sat alone at the bar laughing and joking with the bartender. For a moment, Candace feared interrupting his good time. Nevertheless, she did. She swayed naturally and gracefully. Each movement accentuated her defined waist and large hips. She approached his stool and intentionally brushed his arm with her breasts.

Ibra turned to her, grinning. "You made it."

"You didn't think I was going to?" she asked.

"I'm just glad you did. You returned to me," he said.

Ibra stood and gave her a tight hug. It was more like they had known each other forever, not just the last three hours.

"You are gorgeous," he said. "I love what you're wearing. But next time not so tight, okay?" He patted her lightly on her rear.

The bartender interrupted. "What would you like ma'am?"

Candace was ready for a drink and had already decided what she wanted. "I'd like—"

"I got this," Ibra said, holding his hand up to her face. "The lady would like a whiskey sour. How's that?" he asked turning to her.

Slightly taken aback, she said, "Fine for me."

Ibra chatted about the end of the event, but Candace barely heard him. She was staring at this wonderfully sculpted, beautiful specimen of a man in front of her. The bartender brought the drinks and set them in front of Ibra.

"Here, drink this," Ibra said pushing a glass toward her.

"Wow, that's a little strong," Candace said, pushing the drink away.

Ibra pulled it back toward her. "Drink it. I didn't see you eat or drink anything tonight. And I was watching. I watched you talk to that ugly woman in the green dress. I watched how you walked around with the same glass of wine but never took a sip. I saw you with that guy with glasses. And I watched you talk to a group of young ladies. You laughed a lot during that one."

Candace scowled and tried to be offended, but she couldn't hide the fact that she really enjoyed Ibra's attention. She softened her eyebrows and stared at him.

"How about a little pineapple juice?" she pleaded.

"Would you add some in there for her, please?" Ibra asked the bartender.

As she drank, they continued the conversation. Ibra told tales of his career and the years that led him to law school.

"So, where is your family from?" Candace asked.

"My family? We are local. Not too far from here. I basically grew up at a boarding school, so my boarding school family is more like family to me." He smiled and leaned in and stroked her cheek.

"What about you, Candace? Where is your family from? You have a lovely, exotic look. You don't look like the women from around here. Did you come here for school? For college?" His questions confirmed his interest and Candace loved every bit of it.

He outlined her face gently with his fingers as he spoke.

"I'm from here. But my family is Nigerian. I went to NYU," she said, although clearly caught up in his touch.

"Wonderful. Ethnic, intelligent, and drop-dead gorgeous."

"Mmmm. Thank you," she said seductively. "Tell me, Ibra, when you say exotic, what do you mean?"

Candace moved in closer to his face as she spoke. She was close enough to feel him breathing on her. Without any more words, Ibra took her face and kissed her passionately. His hands caressed the back of her neck and crept to her scalp. He untangled her luxurious curls and pulled on them lightly. He kissed her even more passionately, this time taking a handful of her hair in his. He yanked her head back as he leaned in toward her. Candace pushed away.

"Okay that's enough for now," she said wiping her mouth and looking around sheepishly.

Ibra stared at her. "Would you like something to eat? I'm sure you're hungry. This beautiful body of yours can't stay so small. I feel like I need to fatten you up."

Candace laughed, slightly uncomfortable. "I'll just have fries or something, whatever you're having."

Ibra shook his head. "Me? No, I won't eat or drink right now. I have to make sure I'm completely alert."

"My friend, get her another one of these please." He pointed at the bartender and tapped the glass.

Candace protested. "I haven't finished this one yet, Ibra."

"Don't worry, you will," he responded.

They sat around a little longer, although Ibra didn't touch an alcoholic beverage or a morsel of food. He massaged Candace's neck and shoulders as she ate. She returned the favor by caressing his chest and outlining his abs through his tailored shirt.

"Last call!" the bartender bellowed and busied himself with the rush of final drink orders.

"Oh my God, is it that time already?" said Candace. "Time flies, huh?"

Ibra agreed, leaned in, and kissed her forehead.

"Let's do this again. What are you doing, say tomorrow night?" he asked playing with her hair.

"I'm free," Candace said quickly.

He leaned in again and kissed her, allowing his hands to fall from her hair back to her shoulders. He kissed her deeply and his fingers crept toward her neck.

The bartender interrupted them. "Buddy, we're about to wrap up now."

"Yeah sure," Ibra said. "I'll take care of this."

The bartender returned quickly with a bill.

"Candace, I can't wait to see you tomorrow." As he spoke, he forcefully pulled the crevice of her blouse down exposing the top of her breasts. Candace slapped his hand and quickly adjusted herself, embarrassed.

He whispered through clenched teeth, "Don't ever do that again." Then he hugged her warmly, forcing her head to his neck. Candace assented and allowed her body to fall into his.

"Let me walk you to your car," he said, moving her in the direction of the door. "How do you feel about getting dressed up tomorrow night? I have the perfect place to take you. A woman of your caliber should be wined and dined and serviced regularly."

Candace couldn't help but show her excitement. "I can't wait," she said. "I know you're a busy man, but if you're up, text me tonight."

✠✠

CHAPTER 22: BACK TO THE CAPITOL

Mina woke early and decided to head to the capitol before the midday rush. She had barely pulled into the parking lot when she noticed the car right beside hers was Senator Kingsly's. He sat in the driver's seat talking aggressively to someone on speaker. Although she wasn't able to hear him, his affect told a different story. He flailed his arms and punched the steering wheel a few times. She tried hard not to stare but was unsuccessful. He seemed close to her in age, but his face had much more wear and tear. She saw that he could be handsome, and at one point, he probably was. She wondered what weights he had been carrying that prematurely aged him. When he saw her, he quickly composed himself. Within moments, he was out of the car and had locked it behind him. He looked at Mina and waved.

"Mrs. Blake," he said as she opened her door. "Are you headed my way?"

Mina's legs started to shake as she stood up. She suddenly had a case of nerves. "I'm going back to Oren's desk. I believe some things were left behind."

He offered his arm to walk with her. In light of her wobble, she accepted it.

"Is there anything in particular you are looking for? Maybe I can help you," he said.

"You're a godsend," Mina responded followed by a deep sigh. "There were some photos that he kept on his work computer. I wonder if you can help me gain access to those."

She threw more weight into her stroll with the senator, leaning on him a bit.

He nodded in agreement. "Oh, I understand. I wouldn't want to lose those either. I don't believe that IT has taken his computer or wiped it yet. Why don't I walk you over there and we can see for ourselves?

"I would really appreciate that, Senator Kingsly."

Each step she took was stronger and more deliberate.

Mina heard a voice whisper in her ear, "You are strong, ya hear? Strong."

"What, Senator?" Mina asked.

"I didn't say anything," he replied.

She released his arm and walked upright, matching the senator stride for stride.

He walked her to the second floor and into the IT office.

"Young man, please locate the computer of Senator Oren Blake. His widow is here and would like to retrieve personal items from it."

Without raising his head, a young intern replied "Okay. Leave her name and I'll see if one of the guys can look into it."

Senator Kingsly leaned into the desk where the intern sat. "Young man, do not trifle with me. You're going to do this for Mrs. Blake immediately. We will wait and I have zero tolerance for ineptness. Let us not forget that I am personally acquainted with your manager."

The intern lifted his head abruptly and choked out a response. "Senator Kingsly! Oh! Okay. It will only be a moment for us to retrieve it from the back office."

When the young man returned with Oren's laptop, Senator Kingsly left Mina to her business.

She began logging on in the same fashion that she had on the home laptop. Password: 0628. She was in.

Initially the intern hovered. At one point, the young man perched himself right at Mina's shoulder.

"You may go now," she said dismissively, "unless you want me to call Senator Kingsly back."

The intern hustled back to his chair.

Oren's computer had the familiar files on it. Mina scrolled through his events, itineraries, letters, and the like. She did find a very large file with pictures of him and his colleagues and of course him and his love. A nondescript file labeled: RESEARCH appeared toward the end of his documents file. Mina opened it. She found online articles, links, news briefs, and private investigator reports.

Oren had been uncovering a story amassed over the four neighboring states confirming professional women who had gone missing. The private investigator had traced the private lives of a number of women who were currently reported missing. It had details of their work, their social habits, their boyfriends and girlfriends, their consumption of alcohol, and other questionable behavior. The final documents seemed to be the most helpful: affidavits of the last people these women were seen with prior to their disappearances. Mina expected that the last person would have been friends or family members. However, in all of the cases, the family members reported that their loved ones had frequented a bar or a party and were expected home shortly thereafter. There were virtually no reports or firsthand accounts of who they spent time with at the bar or party. Mina read the transcript from the local news briefs. They were from neighboring states; all outlined that a number of women from their towns had gone missing.

The final discovery produced saved travel vouchers and itineraries that were not Oren's. Mina started to get suspicious. *Why would my husband need to have the travel arrangements for someone else?*

Mina knew that as a junior senator there were many activities Oren had to endure for which he was overqualified. Travel consultant to the more seasoned senators was one. It served Mina well in this case, because sitting right on his computer were the travel arrangements for Senator Sam Kingsly and his coordinating itineraries. There were conferences, symposia, dinners, and banquets. Senator Sam Kingsly was a busy man and did much of his traveling at the expense of the state. Upon quick perusal, Mina was able to link up the dates and destinations when the senator had been traveling. Coincidentally, his travel destinations coincided with the town briefs Mina read about. She knew she'd have to dig deeper to figure out if the travel dates aligned. There was no time for that today. She hurriedly copied all that she could find before the intern got up enough courage to approach her again.

✠✠

CHAPTER 23: GREAT DISCOVERY

In the car, Mina called Detective Toure. "Detective, I really need to see you."

They met at the same coffee shop as usual. Detective Toure looked concerned and fiddled with his glasses as he slid into the booth.

"I rushed right over here, Mrs. Blake. What's going on? Are you all right? Is it Candace?"

"Wow. You really did take a liking to her didn't you?" she asked. "How was last night?"

The detective looked puzzled. "What do you mean? It was fine, nothing out of the ordinary."

"Oh no? Are late-night drinks nothing out of the ordinary?" Mina asked.

"I don't know what you're talking about, Mrs. Blake. Honestly," the detective retorted.

"Never mind then. I was only asking." Mina huffed and folded her arms.

After neither of them spoke for a few awkward moments, Mina broke the silence. "This is what I wanted to talk to you about. It's Senator Kingsly. Oren found a correlation between his travel and the women's disappearances. This spans four states. I think we have a madman on our hands."

"Another one?" asked Detective Toure, sounding exasperated.

"I know it's all connected," said Mina. "I'm not sure how, but I'm looking into it. I have to get close to him. But I don't know how."

"Close to whom?" the detective demanded. "Senator Kingsly?"

Mina narrowed her eyes as she responded, "If Senator Kingsly is a kidnapping serial rapist who killed my husband, I will hunt him down and meticulously destroy him: life, breath, and all."

"Now, Mrs. Blake..." the detective started.

"Look here, Detective, I'm as serious as every breath in my body! But don't mistake my resolve for emotion. Ancient warrior women were known to sleep with their conquests by night and have them executed in the morning. Trust and believe, I will ruin his career, defame his character, and ensure that he is abused every moment that he is in prison."

The detective reluctantly interrupted Mina's tirade. "Let me get this straight. You're actually considering getting close to him? And what if he is a sadistic rapist like you think—that means that you're next."

Mina's eyes lacked compassion or tenderness. Her words were cold. "Don't worry about me. I'm ready for him and that misogynistic bull. I'm no saint."

Detective Toure was visibly shocked at Mina's static grin.

"Meanwhile, you really have to find out more, Detective," she continued. "I have so many questions. What is it about these women that we're missing? Is there a connection? Is it random? Why them and why now?"

The detective nodded, knitting his brows in concern. "There is definitely something going on with the senator," he said. "So, does that mean that you're no longer considering Attorney Marcus as the man who killed your husband?"

"I wouldn't go that far. I just don't know," Mina said. "But I know that these men are not fit to lead," she continued decisively. "They're holding secrets and that secret cost Oren his life."

✠✠

CHAPTER 24: KNOCKOUT

Once she got home, Mina called out for Candace but there was no response. Disappointed, she paced from room to room unable to contain her energy. She felt resilient and wanted to share it with her best friend.

More importantly, Mina felt ready. She craved more knowledge about herself and felt the void of ignorance. She knew she was different, but that's all she knew. She wasn't sure if it was energy, adrenaline, resolve, or something greater. But whatever it was coursed like fire through her veins in a way that nothing else ever had before.

She darted around her home for a few more minutes before determining that she couldn't stay there. She jumped into her car and allowed her mind to wander as she drove aimlessly. She pulled into a parking lot to find that she was at Knockout Gym.

When she walked through the door, Mina behaved as though she knew where she was going and had been there a thousand times over. A short woman with exceptionally well-defined muscles greeted her at the door.

"May I help you?" she asked politely yet firmly.

"I'm here to see Kimber. I'm Mina. She invited me a few days ago."

"Oh, *you're* Mina," the woman responded folding her arms across her chest. "I've heard about you. I heard it was some exhibition you guys put on that night. Kimber couldn't stop gushing about it. She said that was the most fun she's had in a really long time. Anywho, follow me."

She led her down the hall to a wide, open room. It was well lit and the best reggae dance hall music boomed through the speakers.

An older man dressed in all black spandex approached her first. "And who might you be?" he asked, giving Mina a blank stare. His voice was deep and steady.

"Oh my God! Mina! You came." Kimber rushed over wearing gloves and protective gear. She gave Mina a big hug, confirming the immediate friendship that Mina suspected they had.

"I wasn't sure you'd come. But I just felt it. Just like I felt the instant vibe when we met." Kimber's words flew fast. "How you doing?" she asked excitedly, jumping up and down.

Mina shared Kimber's excitement and was bubblier than she'd been in a long time. "Oh, I'm just fine. I was hoping to get some more tips from you, though. I'm coming up on some things and I want to make sure I'm ready. And I could consider no better person than you," Mina said.

"Most definitely! You're already a part of my tribe." Kimber engulfed Mina in another bear hug. Without a second to spare, Kimber took the older man's hands and placed them in Mina's.

"Here. Meet my trainer. Like I told you, your form of Capoeira is close to his. I've only ever seen it done properly here at Knockout. Go ahead, Mina, show him," Kimber said.

Mina was petrified. In her head, she knew nothing about this art and fighting form. She held onto her belly and felt the warmth as it moved quickly from her stomach up to her extremities and outward again. Once her body filled with that warmth, her mind was transformed in a way she could not explain. Giving it no further thought, Mina moved naturally into action. She glided from one movement to the other and gracefully slid across the floor in circles to a beat in her own head. She heard the sound of drums from a distance. She danced to them and kicked and swayed and landed cartwheels and roundhouses. She did what she felt, and she felt everything. When the drums stopped, she stopped. She paused and stood in front of Kimber and the trainer. Bowing, she returned to fighting stance.

Kimber nudged her trainer. "Didn't I tell you? Wasn't that stupendous?"

The trainer clapped slowly and with intention; he was captivated. Mina nodded her head in thanks but remained standing where she was.

"Where did you learn that?" the trainer asked.

Mina relaxed her stance and spoke thoughtfully. "Truthfully, I really don't know. I felt it and I followed the drums."

The trainer gestured wildly and clapped with new enthusiasm. "That's exactly what I'm talking about! That's when you know is authentic." His deep voice resonated within Mina's slender frame. He placed a heavy hand on her shoulder. "You know you are an old soul, don't you? This isn't your first merry-go-round."

"Well, that's what I'm hearing," Mina responded.

"Tell me about what you're hearing," the trainer said, thoroughly intrigued.

"Huh, okay. Where to start? My name is Aminatu," she began.

"Stop right there!" The trainer was so pleased with this discovery he rocked back and forth on his heels. "The Warrior Queen should know the dance of the warrior."

Mina was tickled by his response. Her eyes twinkled as she spoke. "You've heard my name before?"

"Oh yes," the trainer responded. "My parents were staunch believers in informing me of my heritage. It's rich."

He turned to Kimber. "Kimby, let's switch it up for a moment since we have a guest. Show Aminatu the moves of the warrior. You say something is coming up? You'll be ready."

"Now," he instructed, "begin."

Before the session was over, Mina progressed and in that short period of time, she became more and more advanced.

"It's like it comes to you intuitively," Kimber said, beaming. "I could work with you all day, Mina."

"I want to know more," Mina responded. "So, maybe you'll get that chance." She laughed and winked.

Kimber reached up to give her a high five. "Be here tomorrow okay?" It was more of a command than a question.

"Yes, ma'am. Don't want to anger the champion. Sure will." Mina responded as she headed toward the door.

She drove home, feeling a bit lighter. When she arrived, there was no sign of Candace. Mina found dishes washed and stacked in the dish rack. The living room had been tidied up. The bathroom reeked of bleach. And there was food cooked on the stove already. All of this, but no Candace. Hungry from her workout, Mina helped herself to the food and sat down to enjoy.

✠✠
CHAPTER 25: DINNER

"Beautiful, you look radiant tonight," Ibra said as he opened the door for Candace.

"You're so sweet. I wore this for you," she said, standing and twirling.

"You already know what I like. Not too tight but hugs all your bodacious curves," Ibra stated matter-of-factly.

Candace blushed and nodded. Ibra offered his arm for support as he led her into the restaurant. Although Candace was an interior designer and well acquainted with classy, this was the most upscale dining venue she had ever seen. She did not hide her awe as they walked in and were seated.

"Attorney Marcus, we have your booth ready." The maître d' beckoned them to follow him. He handed them off to the head waiter who stood nearby, waiting to receive them.

"Your first course will be out momentarily," said the waiter.

Ibra walked to Candace's seat, holding it out for her and helping her get settled. He lifted her chin and kissed her affectionately on the lips.

"Prepare to have a great night," he said with the greatest conviction.

"I already am," Candace said, swooning.

Their meals were selected without any input from Candace. Ibra preordered everything for her. Unbeknownst to him she had no allergies or aversions. Candace didn't think it would have mattered to Ibra if she did anyway.

"Tell me more about you, Ibra," she said.

"You don't need to know anything more about me." He spoke definitively and sternly. "You know all you need to know."

Seeing Candace's face, he softened his tone.

"I will tell you this—I treat my women well. I will wine you and dine you and treat you like the queen that you are. But don't take me for granted. Naughty girls that do that receive punishment from Daddy."

Candace was taken aback yet again but tried not to show it. Instead, she thrust some salad in her mouth and chewed so she could not respond.

"I brought you a present," he said, fishing in his pocket. He produced a glimmering, shiny gold tennis bracelet. He walked over and fastened it around Candace's arm.

"There you go," he said contentedly. "Just the way I like it."

He leaned down and kissed her again, this time biting her lip just a little.

"Ouch," she said and pulled away. "Don't do that, Ibra."

Smirking, he walked back to his seat. During the meal, local reporters came up and asked to take their picture, but Ibra waved them off. Women stared at him from everywhere in the restaurant. Candace saw their eyes and recognized their hungry stares; they wanted him. Despite the attention, Candace was quite the diva that evening and she knew it. Young and old men made eye contact with her as she visually scrolled the room.

"Oh, they're looking at you, aren't they?" Ibra asked annoyed.

"Perhaps," Candace responded. "If they weren't, wouldn't you be concerned that I'm not worth looking at?"

Ibra relaxed and laughed. "True. And you are quite stunning. They can look all they want, but I have the pleasure of being in your company tonight. You're mine."

At that, Candace relaxed as well. They continued to chat about little things throughout the night. Candace was enthralled with Ibra. And she made him laugh.

"I'm going to a conference tomorrow. Why don't you come with me? It'd be a great chance to get to know you a little better. You can stay in the hotel and get anything your heart desires. Come. It's on me," he said insistently.

"I don't know what to say. We've only just met, Ibra," Candace responded.

"It doesn't matter how long I've known you, Candace. I know what I want. And by the way, I get what I want." He smiled a big disarming smile as he spoke.

"Tell you what," Mina interjected, "I'll tell you tonight after I get home. Is that too late?"

"Just tell me now. Tell me that my driver can pick you up in the morning and that we'll fly out tomorrow as well." He was almost begging.

"I'm not sure about all this. But I'll tell you tonight," she said.

Ibra pouted and Candace pretended not to notice. The waiter brought the dessert and coffee.

"Don't drink the coffee," Ibra demanded. "Have water.

"Why?" Candace asked innocently.

Ibra responded, "Because then you will taste like coffee when I kiss you. And I'm going to kiss you."

Candace obliged and pushed the coffee back reaching for the water instead.

"Why don't we go by my place for a little while tonight?" he asked.

Contemplating it, Candace shook her head.

"Come on, baby. Just do what Daddy asks," Ibra insisted.

"Just for a short while?" Candace asked. "You'll make sure to drop me home?"

"Absolutely. I'll take good care of you tonight," he assured her.

"Well…" she started.

Candace's phone vibrated in her purse. She reached for the phone.

"Don't get that. Not now," Ibra said, his voice firm.

Candace checked the number and saw that it was Mina.

"This is my best friend. Just give me one second," she said.

"No!" Ibra slammed his fist hard on the table. "Not now," he said gritting his teeth.

Candace jumped back startled. Her heart raced and she looked around to find the entire restaurant staring at them. She silenced her phone and put it back in her purse.

Ibra reached out for her hands. "I'm sorry, beautiful, but I just can't have your attention diverted right now. Come on, I'll get the check and we'll change the scenery." His voice was softer now.

Her phone rang again. She went to answer it and felt his tight grip on her arm. He whispered harshly, "Not now!"

Candace wriggled away and shoved her phone back in her purse.

Ibra called the waiter over and complimented him on his service that evening. As he spoke, he pulled out his wallet and paid for their meal. Seizing the opportunity while he was distracted, Candace opened her phone and sent a quick text.

He shifted his gaze from the check and looked at her. "I need your full attention tonight, beautiful."

Candace felt her purse as a response text came in. She held it tightly to draw no attention to it. Shaking inwardly, she leaned in to Ibra. "Listen, babe, let me run to the ladies' room. Get myself right for you."

Ibra nuzzled her neck and kissed her intently until she pulled away. "You know I'm falling in love with you," he said. "Go ahead. I'll be at the front waiting for you with our driver."

Candace gracefully swayed and swished all the way to the ladies' lounge. In the restroom, she checked the bottom of each stall to ensure she was alone. She went into the last stall and grabbed her phone and dialed immediately.

"Mina," Candace whispered.

"Candy!" Mina sounded distraught. "I'll be there in four minutes. Buy me time."

Candace knew she could distract Ibra for five minutes, allowing time for Mina to pull up. She stayed in the lounge for precisely four minutes. Taking her time, she walked out of the ladies' lounge and made her way to the front of the restaurant.

Ibra was waiting just as he said he would. He leaned on the car and his driver was poised and ready. He looked exceptionally sexy—so polished and well refined. Candace was drawn to him and kept her eyes fixed intently on him.

"I hope you know how gorgeous you are tonight," Ibra called out to her as she walked.

Candace smiled and walked quickly toward him. She gave him a long hug and an even longer kiss. He grabbed her waist and pulled her close, holding tightly to her clothing.

Just then, Mina pulled up behind them. In the darkness of the evening, all anyone could see was her car's headlights. Mina pulled her baseball cap lower to shield her face.

Candace loosened herself from Ibra's grasp. "Look, babe, I'm sorry I have to pass tonight. Emergency at home," she said as she started walking toward Mina.

Ibra snatched Candace back. "What!" he said, his voice almost a growl. His face was contorted, his eyes wide, and he stood up straight in a defensive position. That's when he lifted his hand to strike her.

"No!" Candace yelled.

Mina watched as Candace yanked her arm free from the man's grip and she ran to Mina's car before he had a chance to say or do anything more. Candace hurried inside and closed the door swiftly behind her.

Wasting no time, Mina peeled out of the restaurant's circular driveway, whipping past the stranger's car. They made it a few miles down the road where theirs was the only car to be seen.

"Sweetie, what is going on?" Mina asked. She felt jumpy with worry. "Who was that man?" She reached out and held Candace's hand, noticing her friend was shaking.

Candace remained silent, her breath coming in bursts.

But there was no need for Candace to relay what happened. In an instant, Mina felt everything about the last two nights. A warmth grew inside her, starting from her chest and radiating outward. Overwhelmed, she pulled her hand from Candace and firmly gripped the steering wheel. She was no longer able to focus on the road and driving was the furthest thing from her mind. Breaking out into a cold sweat, a mixture of lust, desire, fear, and loathing overcame Mina all at the same time. She started to shake, unable to distance herself from the powerful emotions. As she shook, the car swerved and accelerated. The acceleration whipped both Mina and Candace back and Mina continued to convulse.

"Mina!" Candace screamed from the passenger seat. "Mina!"

The car was headed directly into a guardrail that was only feet away at high speed. Mina shook viciously but again tried to gain control of her car. She yelled at the top of her lungs,

"Eshu!"

Seconds away from impact, the car jerked to the left, completely straightening itself out. It abruptly came to a stop.

Thoroughly hyperventilating, Mina fumbled to open the door and fell to the ground. She doubled over holding on to her knees for support as she rocked back and forth. All she could whisper was "Thank you," repeatedly. She managed to breathe in and out for a few seconds while glancing back at the car. Candace remained in the passenger seat, a look of shock and horror on her face.

Mina inched herself back into the car and slowly put it into gear. Home was not far away. They crept along the road ensuring that the slow ride home was without additional incident. Once safely in the driveway, Mina withdrew her keys and took several quick shallow breaths. She sat there in the driveway and sobbed. Her wailing was so intense she needed the steering wheel to support her head.

"Candy," she said, unable to mask her grief, "you were supposed to die tonight."

***

Candace and Mina curled up together on the couch, hugging each other tightly. For those moments, they were inseparable. Their feet touched, arms linked, and heads rested on each other. When one of them moved out of the way, the other quickly came back into contact. Their contact was intentional; they had been on the brink of loss.

"Why didn't you tell me, Candy?" Mina asked quietly.

"I just couldn't, Mina. He was so...so...so everything I've always wanted," she said.

"But, Candy, I've told you about him. You don't know what he's capable of."

Candace held her head down and the tears began to roll.

"No, Mina. That's not completely accurate. I started to get a little taste." Candace spoke slowly, as though contemplating each word. "He was aggressive. Since we met it was, 'Do this, do that, drink this, wear that.'" Candace whimpered as she spoke. "Oh my God, what was I thinking?" She lay her head in Mina's lap. As Mina played with her hair, separating the strands, Candace continued timidly. "Mina, I have a question."

"Sure. Shoot."

"Why did you say that thing that you said in the car?" Candace's voice trembled.

Mina took a long, deep breath and stopped playing with her hair. "I saw it, Candy. More like, I felt it. I felt what you felt in the car—the lust, the desire, the tension. I felt all that. Then my own emotions comingled with them. But honestly, I felt your life dissipate suddenly. You faded, Candy…took your last breath. I felt…you die."

They both lay in silence unable to let go of one another.

In the wee hours of the morning Candace's phone rang. She studied the unfamiliar number and lifted the phone to answer.

"Don't answer it!" Mina shouted. "It's him."

"But that's not his number," Candace responded.

"Don't do it, Candy. Please," Mina said.

Candace relented, turning the phone off.

✠✠

CHAPTER 26: NEW ASSIGNMENT

Detective Toure waltzed into the chief's office. He rapped on the door before he entered.

"Chief, do you have a moment?" he asked.

The chief responded, seemingly annoyed and appearing very preoccupied, as was his norm. "Make it quick, Toure!" he grunted.

Detective Toure adjusted his glasses. He cleared his throat quite awkwardly. "I want to help with the investigation of the missing women, sir. I'd like to be assigned."

The chief looked up from the paperwork that clearly had his full attention. "What are you working on now?" he asked,

"I was working on the Blake case but that has been transferred," the detective responded.

"Oh yeah, that's right. I need to check in on that one. The deputy chief assured me that it's progressing nicely. Nevertheless, why the sudden interest?" the chief asked.

"Not sudden, sir. But considering this is such a high-profile investigation for the department, I figured you need all hands on deck."

The chief reclined in his seat and tapped his pencil on the desk.

After a few seconds, he spoke up. "You're right about that, Toure. We could use some additional hands. Deputy Chief Lakos is heading this one up. Report to him in the morning. I'll let him know you're also assigned to this case now."

"Thank you, sir. I just want to help." Detective Toure extended his hand to shake the chief's.

"Close the door behind you, Toure." The chief lowered his head and returned to his pile of papers.

The following morning, Detective Toure arrived early and sat outside Deputy Lakos's office. He came prepared. He was nonchalantly sipping his coffee and flipping through a file when the deputy arrived.

The deputy walked down the hall quickly, failing to acknowledge anyone, including the officers who said "Good morning" to him as he entered.

The detective vied for his attention with a hearty, "Good morning, sir!" to which the deputy again failed to respond. "The chief assigned me to the missing women case," the detective stated.

"I'm aware," the deputy responded without looking at Detective Toure or even speaking in his direction. With his back turned, he opened his office door and went inside.

Not waiting for an invitation, Detective Toure followed him in. "I have some thoughts on how to continue this investigation."

Annoyed, the deputy turned to face him. His statement was terse and colored with disdain. "You walk in here with some ideas, not even considering that I've been working this case for months. Your disrespect *will not* fly in here. Forget it. Get out. *Now.*" The deputy held the door open and gestured for the detective to leave.

"That's not what I meant, Deputy!" the detective said, protesting. "I was thinking of different angles on how I can be most effective. I got a chance to look through the file. I've been studying ad nauseam."

"Listen. I don't care what you've been studying. I will tell you what to look at and when. We have a protocol and method of investigation here and either you fall in or go back to investigating the shoplifters at Price Cutters." The deputy got in the detective's face as he spoke.

Detective Toure's armpits became sweaty and his forehead grew warm. "However you need me to help, sir. That's why I'm here."

The deputy stepped away from the detective. "That's more like it. You can stand to be a little more humble. Work on that."

The deputy sat at his desk. "Have a seat. This is what I was considering. The newest missing woman is a law school professor from the neighboring town. She has been missing for two weeks. The woman before her has been missing now for one month. She's a pediatrician from our city. These missing persons cases have really started to ramp up. I don't know what is happening, but our citizens are getting scared and the governor is coming down on us. So, if you're going to help, this is what I need you to do. Stick to me and let me teach you a thing or two."

The detective stared at him, expressionless, but the deputy kept speaking. "These are the rules: Where I go, you go. Don't run off all rogue, either. Can't believe the chief has me working with…you" He sighed and mumbled under his breath. "In the meantime, find out everything there is to know about the missing doctor. Her background, her habits, her favorite color. Everything."

The deputy shoved an additional two files at Detective Toure. "I'll be looking into the professor's disappearance."

Detective Toure sat and started to flip through the files.

But Deputy Lakos shook his head *No* while staring at the detective. "Not here. Anywhere but here. I'll come get you when it's time to go out in the field."

Detective Toure stood abruptly. The deputy shooed him out the door and began to close it before he'd even left.

Standing outside the office, Detective Toure heard Deputy Lakos pick up the phone.

"Hey. We need to talk. Tonight. I don't care where you will be. Tonight."

Detective Toure heard the sound of the phone being slammed down and the deputy's footsteps as he moved closer toward the closed door. Detective Toure scurried away quickly to get out of the vicinity.

Back at his desk, the detective carefully went through the files in front of him. The missing woman he was looking into was a recent med school graduate and had just passed her medical boards. She had been in practice for about six months and was a sole practitioner. She was single and attractive, something all the women seemed to have in common.

She was reported missing after returning from a national pediatric medicine conference. The file showed she'd been scheduled to arrive back home on Wednesday the ninth. Her flight was on time and she was on it. That was the last time she was seen.

According to the reports, her family said that she had a dinner scheduled with them that Friday evening. They thought nothing of it when they didn't hear from her before then. When she didn't show up, her parents called her cell phone and left many messages but still were not alarmed. It was customary that when the doctor was entrenched in work she would shut the rest of her family and friends out. The following morning, her brothers stopped by her home and did not see her car. Even her best friend had not heard from her in a few days. It wasn't until an additional three days passed that the family reported her missing.

Detective Toure closed the file, perplexed. These women were accomplished, single, and exceptionally pretty. Whoever was preying on them recognized a weakness, exploited it, and was suave enough to lure them away. He couldn't imagine how these women were all falling prey to someone or something.

"I really pray they're alive," Detective Toure said out loud.

***

Mina flipped a business card over in her hand: from finger to thumb and then to the other hand, from finger to thumb. Her breathing got more rapid and her heart thundered a bit. She gazed at the corner of her bedroom where she had constructed her first altar.

"Ancestors, this is where I need you. Show me. I'm ready. Guide me. Let me discern the truth." Mina closed her eyes. "Eshu, you helped me once. I need you once more."

She felt the familiar warmth in her belly. The warmth turned into a fire that rested in her being. She let down her locks and flipped her head from side to side. She felt mighty, unstoppable.

When Mina looked in the mirror, instead of her own reflection she saw an unfamiliar one. She was enamored with the woman staring back at her but not scared. Mina carefully examined her features. The woman smiled sweetly and although Mina was nervous, she smiled back. She wasn't sure if she was that woman and that woman was her or if it was something much more than that. Mina opened her mouth to talk, but the woman did not. Taken aback but too curious to walk away, Mina stared at the woman in front of her.

She had beautifully dark skin chiseled right out of a cacao bean and was wide-eyed and confident in her expression. Wounds and scars on her face added dimension and an attractiveness that Mina had never seen before. A small indented scar told a tale of many years gone by. It was over her eye and hidden within her eyebrow yet distinct enough to be recognizable.

Her chocolate skin and high cheekbones held a
perfection reserved only for a sculptor. Her lips were
full and dark brown. Her nose was wide, contouring
outward; it complemented the slenderness of her face.
The base of her chin revealed a scar likely from a
knife wound. Yet even with her scars, she was
breathtakingly beautiful.

Her entire essence exuded her passion, desire,
and ability. She was adorned appropriately as well.
Mina could only see her from her shoulders up, but
that was all that she needed to see. Her jewelry was
exquisite, not from this time or space. Her earrings
were a precious metal, likely silver, Mina surmised,
but she wasn't sure. The necklace was an ornate piece
of battered gold. It narrowed and spanned her entire
neckline, wrapping around her neck multiple times.
The many layers each had a separate character but
revealed a consistency. Hanging from the center of
the necklace was a unique piece. Mina cocked her
head to one side and saw that her reflection did the
same. Mina lifted her own necklace, which consisted
of a single gold chain and a charm. Mimicking that,
her reflection lifted the ornate piece that hung from
her neck as well. Examining the piece in the mirror,
Mina saw the same half circle wavy charm that she
wore. She looked down to confirm with her own eyes:
identical.

Mina opened her mouth intent on asking one question. All she was able to get out was her own mouthing of the words "Who are you?" The reflection echoed the same a moment later. *Who are you? Who are you?*

Dumbfounded, Mina stood there, unsure and confused. She stared back at the reflection and marveled that she looked so strong and confident. A sense of inferiority consumed her. *I don't know who I am. I don't know why this is me,* she thought. A few tears seeped out of the corners of her eyes. The reflection stared at her with kindness yet intensity. "You are strong, ya hear," she mouthed and Mina nodded and accepted every word.

Feeling for the pendant key that hung from her neck, Mina looked down and examined it, thoroughly memorizing the intricacies of the pattern. She looked back up and saw that the woman in the reflection was gone. In the mirror, Mina saw herself but enhanced with newly adorned locks and a slight hint of fire in her eyes.

No way, thought Mina. *There's no way!*

Her eyes changed hues. Once beautiful, big and brown, they were now closer to hazel. They twinkled when she looked at them. She really did have a fire in her eyes.

✠

CHAPTER 27: CONTACT

"Senator Kingsly, this is Aminatu Blake," Mina spoke into the phone.

"Mrs. Blake, to what do I owe this honor?" Senator Kingsly replied.

"I hope you don't think this is too forward but I was hoping you would be free this evening. I need someone to talk to who understood my husband's world."

"Of course I can meet with you. I'd be happy to be of service."

"How does dinner sound to you? Around seven," Mina said.

Mina agonized over getting ready in a way she hadn't in a long time. She picked out a dress that highlighted and accentuated all her best parts. She was careful to do her makeup allowing her newly hazel eyes to shine brightly with that color palette. Her hair was piled in a lovely little updo that showed off the curves of her face. Fascinated with the color red, Mina chose a pair of strappy red heels. She looked like she was about both business and pleasure.

She'd orchestrated the meeting with the senator at a plush restaurant just out of town. It was surprising when, for whatever reason, Senator Kingsly jumped at the opportunity. Mina was determined to ensure that she received every piece of information she could get out of him. She didn't care how she did it or who she ran through to get it. Mina was entering the warrior zone. Still weighing the senator's possible involvement in Oren's death, she had no qualms about annihilating him.

"Mrs. Blake," the senator began, "you look simply amazing."

Mina had just exited her car where both the valet and the senator were waiting. She spun around, sure to expose just a hint of her perfectly fit body.

"Thank you," she responded. "It was really good of you to come out at my beck and call tonight."

"It's my pleasure. It's not every day that a goddess invites me out," the senator joked.

As he reached out his hand for hers, Mina marveled at how truly attractive he was. He was weathered for sure, but he looked confident now, as opposed to simply worn. He was obviously a details man. Everything had to be just right. Mina could tell: His cuff links were expensive—gold and onyx. His suit was obviously tailored. The senator was not tall; he appeared average in height. Mina was able to look right into his eyes with her heels on. He was evidently very good at being a politician; his presence was larger than his physical body. Mina was sure that everyone saw them when they walked into the room and she liked it.

Despite her initial inclination, Mina didn't come on strong during dinner. She sensed that patience was going to be the key here. And she was determined to execute her plan successfully.

Senator Kingsly was polite and gracious. As a politician, he clearly had a way with words and topics. He avoided any controversial subjects. He was a good date, although Mina strategically plotted his demise the entire time.

"Why have we never met before?" Mina asked. "Didn't you work with my husband?

"Well, we sat across the aisle. He had his party and I had mine. But because of our work on the confirmation committee, we did know of each other," he said.

"Confirmation? Yeah, those were the projects that Oren was working on." Mina managed to converse all the while cursing the senator's very existence.

"Do you really want to talk about my work?" he asked. "I assumed tonight you just needed a breather and maybe wanted a friendly face and space to talk."

Mina was nearly struck by his genuine appeal. In some ways, she was tempted to talk, but she could not lose sight of her true intent.

"I'd really like to hear more about you. I feel that there was so much of my husband's life I was not able to share because of the nature of the Senate. This is your opportunity to give the Senate a better reputation. You realize that you guys are known for being stuffy and a little unwavering." Mina laughed.

The senator also laughed and flashed his megawatt smile. "Stuffy? That's the last thing I am. According to my ex-wife, I was a little bit too…let's call it loose." He laughed again.

"So you're not married?" Mina asked.

"No, not anymore. I'm happily single."

"Looking?" Mina's eyes twinkled as she asked.

"Not intentionally," he said with a grin.

"Is it because of work? Do you work too much to have a relationship?" Mina asked.

"You certainly don't waste any time or mince words," he responded. "Are you always this direct?"

Mina chuckled. "Life is short. Why waste your time on pleasantries? I know what I'm looking for."

"Should I assume that means that you have questions for me?" he asked.

"Some. But they can wait for our next get-together."

"There's going to be another get-together, huh?" the senator asked licking his lips.

"Most certainly," Mina replied.

***

"Detective, I'm getting impatient," Mina said, gripping her phone tightly. "It's been weeks since I've heard about my husband's case. I realize that we're all trying to get different angles, but what is your department doing? I just don't understand. I'm going to reach out to the chief."

"No, Mrs. Blake. I don't recommend that," Detective Toure said.

"I'm sorry, Detective but I don't understand *No*," Mina said. "This is just a courtesy call so when you see me at the precinct, you'll know what's going on."

"Wait, Mrs. Blake—"

She hung up without letting him continue.

Later that morning at the precinct, Mina stood and waited patiently in the reception area.

"I'm here to see Chief Lakos," Mina said dryly to the older gentleman who sat behind the desk.

"I'm sorry, ma'am. Is he expecting you?" he asked.

"No, he is not. But I need to see him immediately."

"The chief is really tied up today, ma'am," the gentleman continued.

"Sir, I don't think you understand." Mina's voice grew louder as she spoke. "Please let him know that Mrs. Aminatu Cisse Blake is here and his attention is required immediately!" Although loud, Mina smiled, batting those hazel eyes. Then she added a flirtatious wink. "I'm happy to wait. I'm sure he must leave the office at some point. I'll wait right here."

Mina planted her feet and did not move. She was exceptionally controlled and confident. The business suit that she wore flattered her. She tapped her feet lightly but her stilettos made quite a significant echo.

Within moments, the chief emerged.

"And you are Mrs. Blake?" he asked, extending his hand.

"I am. But you should know that since you're handling my husband's case," she said, making no attempt to stifle her displeasure.

Sensing her annoyance, the chief turned, retreating back down the hallway. "Come this way," he said quickly.

He was moving fast, but Mina was right there, neck and neck; she met his stride despite her stilettos.

The chief opened his office door and escorted her in. "How may I help you, Mrs. Blake?"

"I'm here to see what progress has been made. I truly expected a call or other correspondence, but I see that my presence is necessary," Mina said.

"Mrs. Blake," the chief began as he closed the door to his office, "I do apologize and let me assure you that we are exploring every avenue. You are correct. We should have done something by now. But, I can let you know as soon as we get more information."

Mina glared at him. "Not exactly, Chief," she said. "I need to know the case status as of this precise moment."

"I'm sorry, Mrs. Blake. I cannot give that to you. I am not prepared to share this information yet."

Mina's voice lowered and her eyes narrowed. Her words were barely above a whisper. "I am prepared to share your incompetence with the mayor. Given his personal friendship with my husband, I'm sure he'd be interested in hearing why the chief of police is stalling." Mina took out her phone and pressed one button.

"Good morning, Mayor Dean!" There was a brief pause Mina's end. "I'm quite well, thanks for asking. Unfortunately, I'm calling about the case. I know you desire to honor Oren's memory as do I. Are you able to move it along for me?" There was another pause. "Thanks so much and my regards to Marianne."

The chief started shuffling papers on his desk. A woman buzzed in on his intercom. "Chief, the mayor is on line one for you." The desk phone blinked as the mayor remained on hold.

The chief pulled at his tie as he blurted quickly to Mina, "Your husband's death is at the center of a cover-up scheme. His brakes had been tampered with, causing the collision and ultimate death." The phone's blinking light reflected in his eyes.

"Chief, you tell me nothing I don't already know. I want to know what your investigation has turned up with regard to motive and suspect. Who and why, Chief!" Mina leaned across the desk within three inches from his face. "Do not need to tell me that you have no leads."

Mina stood up straight still maintaining complete eye contact. "When can I expect to receive an update? Tomorrow would be preferred. I hope you understand the urgency. Oh, and you should get your phone." Mina looked the chief up and down and sashayed out of his office.

✠✠

CHAPTER 28: THE GOOD DETECTIVE

The precinct hustled and bustled with activity of all kinds. Detective Toure checked the parking lot and the grounds thoroughly but had already missed Mina's visit. He brushed by the chief's office en route to meeting the deputy and heard a series of expletives.

"What the hell does that woman think I should do? Drop everything to solve a case of someone who is clearly dead and gone? We have these women who could still be alive! Selfish and self-centered! And now the mayor is on my back! The last thing we need is the mayor..."

By the sound of it, Mina had already gotten to the chief. Detective Toure kept his distance, confident that because of Mina, heads would roll today. Then there was Deputy Steven Lakos. He was already riding the detective. Detective Toure had no opportunity to think critically or creatively. He was completely stifled: being called to observe or engage in mock situations or retraining. He was clearly under the deputy's thumb. Detective Toure wasn't sure how he would react to the deputy's demeaning nature today. Lakos was rattled—he could feel it.

"Took you long enough," Deputy Lakos mumbled, waiting for him at the car.

They rode for forty-five minutes barely speaking to each other. Detective Toure was relieved that talk radio was on. He couldn't bear to engage in a normal conversation with the deputy. He was well aware that Steven Lakos did not care for him. It didn't matter, though. He was there for one reason and one reason only.

They pulled into the parking lot of a large, abandoned market. It had been one of those superstore chains that went out of business. It was way beyond the city limits and toward the outskirts of the neighboring town. Two local officers were waiting for them. As they parked, one of the officers rapped on the deputy's window beckoning him to come out.

"Officers," the deputy began, "I'm Deputy Lakos and this is Detective Toure. Thank you for meeting us today."

The officers shook hands cordially. The more senior officer, as it seemed, stepped forward. "On the phone, you said that you are interested in our missing person's case as well."

Deputy Lakos nodded his head. "Yes, unfortunately we are investigating a rash of our own and we think there may be links."

"Any way that we can help you, we are more than willing. Rumor has it the governor has called our chief as well."

"Tell me about the woman," Deputy Lakos said.

The more senior office began speaking. "She was last seen leaving her job in the evening. She was the law school's evening dean. Her students said they saw her get into her car because everyone was exiting right about the same time. Her roommate reported she came home, received a phone call, and left again. The roommate wasn't home at the time and they corresponded by phone. The next morning, passersby saw her car right here and called the police. For a few years, this was the spot where people left their abandoned cars. The locals started getting upset about it, so now they call us at the drop of a hat. It's a good thing too because it could have been much longer before we were advised of her disappearance."

Detective Toure started walking around the building, still within earshot, but away from the group.

"Is there anything very significant about this area?" the deputy asked.

"Not really. It was a vibrant shopping center just a few years ago. The owners went bankrupt and it has remained vacant ever since," the junior officer responded.

"I assume your officers searched the premises thoroughly?" the deputy inquired.

"Oh yes, sir. That they did. But they turned up very little. No signs of inhabitants," the senior officer replied.

The deputy's phone rang. "Excuse me one moment." He took a few steps away to take the call and spoke in hushed tones.

Detective Toure asked the officers a few more general questions as the deputy continued his conversation. "Have you had other disappearances similar to this?"

The officers shook their heads looking at each other to confirm. "This is a small suburban town, Detective," the senior officer began. "We don't get a lot of incidents like this. There was one that was remotely similar right about last year, but that's not really worth talking about."

"Wait, what do you mean?" the detective protested.

"There was a young woman who reported being assaulted in a bar in town. But there are plenty of holes in her story. She insists that a very attractive man lured her outside in the hopes of getting some cash for, umm…uhhh…you know what. Then he slapped her around a little bit when she was not compliant. According to the woman, he threatened to take her away and that she would never be seen again if she didn't play ball with him. She was beaten up badly—a bunch of bruises by the time she arrived at the station. But again, she has a reputation for a lot of rough and physical stuff, so who really knows."

The detective nodded and jotted some things down on his pad. "Can I have her name and information anyway? It may serve us in the long run."

"Sure. Good luck in finding her. She's very, let's say, elusive. Her name is Lacey."

Deputy Lakos put his phone back in his pocket and turned back toward the group. "So what were you saying again, Officer? You found nothing in this building right? No remnants, no clues, nothing left over? Just her car right?"

"That's exactly right, Deputy. I'm sorry there's not more to tell. You're welcome to take a look around inside or outside. We'll be waiting here for you."

Lakos and Toure took a cursory look around the perimeter and close up at the windows. They were able to see right in without having to go inside. It looked foreboding enough. And just as the officers said, there was nothing visible or anything that could be identified.

"I've seen enough," the deputy said. "Let's head back."

Detective Toure thanked the officers for their time and prepared himself for a silent drive back to the precinct.

On the way back, he resolved to deal with his discomfort. He knew he wasn't going to get any answers by withdrawing into a cocoon and hiding. He drew on the two psychology classes he had taken as a part of his undergrad program at the community college.

"Deputy, as a senior officer, do you think there is a real evidence-based link in all of these cases? You've had a lot of experience with this. Does this look like other cases you have worked on in your career?"

Looking smug, Lakos nodded knowingly. "You're right. I've had a long career in law enforcement. I've seen a lot and what I haven't seen, the chief has clued me in on. You can't judge a book by its cover. Sometimes, it seems all connected but it's really not. You might think that since the MO is similar that the perpetrator of one is the perpetrator of them all. That's not necessarily the case—not in my experience, at least."

Desperate to keep him talking, the detective continued. "What is it about this case that has you thinking that?"

"Well, for one thing, if you had any experience with real police work you would already know this. But I'll enlighten you. People have certain methods and consistencies. People rarely vary their methods. For example, guys that get off by attacking women might leave a calling card like a scarf or something. And men that lure attractive women are generally attractive too. When you see two different methods, especially for high-stakes cases, you can bet that it's two different people carrying it out. I'm just saying that it's unlikely to be so cut and dry like the governor's manhunt suggests." The deputy kept right on driving, oblivious to much else.

"Do you think we're dealing with a serial killer or serial rapist and we just don't realize it yet?" the detective asked genuinely. He was somewhat perplexed by the deputy's response.

"Regular folks aren't that smart, Detective," the deputy replied dryly. "It takes a lot of forethought to engage in such intense methods of debauchery. I'd suggest some people may do it simply for...sport."

Back at the precinct, Detective Toure wasted no time. The deputy was called out for a meeting, allowing the detective to jump into action immediately. With only a few hours to spare before the deputy asked him to do some mundane task, Detective Toure called Mina.

"Mrs. Blake, what are you doing right now? What say we take a ride out?" he requested.

***

Mina met the detective on the sidewalk outside her home. As quickly as he'd called, she was ready to move.

"Did I make you feel bad yesterday? That your precinct was doing nothing?" Mina asked as he pulled off.

"You can't make me feel bad, Mrs. Blake, because again, I want to do this for you. Get to the bottom of all of this. Actually want to do it for me too. It's high time."

"You never did say where we are headed," she said.

"True," the detective responded. "There's a young lady named Lacey I think we need to meet."

A half hour or so later they pulled up to a desolate-looking part of town. Trash lined the sidewalk of the huge housing complex. Random dogs took over the shared driveways and wandered in the streets. Windows were boarded with cardboard and sealed with tape. There were very few windows with blinds or anything that could be considered blinds.

The detective was perplexed. "She could be in any one of these buildings. The address the officers gave me was pretty vague: 138 Buxon Road. It didn't account for a building or apartment number."

Mina closed her eyes and put her hand on her stomach. She stepped out of the car and walked across the grassy lot. The detective scrambled out of the car and followed her, no questions asked. Mina found her way to the back of a building and looked it up and down. She closed her eyes again and took a long deep breath. She opened the heavy gray fire door of the housing unit and proceeded upstairs one flight and stopped. The detective was right behind her. The heavy door slammed startling him and making a ruckus.

"This is it," Mina said. "Do you have an angle?"

"What do you mean this is it? What do you mean an angle?" the detective asked clearly confused.

"Never mind." Mina knocked at the door right in front of her.

A slender worn woman answered the door.

"Yeah," she said.

Mina spoke up first. "We're looking for Lacey. Is she here?"

The woman stepped away from the door and yelled, "Lacey, someone's here for you."

A short, attractive woman in her twenties came to the door.

"Who are you?" she asked, standing slightly behind the door.

The detective spoke up, "Lacey? We'd like to ask you some questions how about an incident you had a year ago. Would you like to step outside?"

"Incident? I haven't gotten in trouble for anything!" she responded.

"No, you didn't get in trouble. But we understand that a man beat you up real bad and threatened you," Detective Toure said.

"Oh." Lacey looked up and down the hallway. "Why don't you come inside instead."

She seated them on a small modest couch. Mina made sure to sit on the very edge just in case she had to jump up suddenly. She was hesitant to let her clothes touch the substances on the couch. She considered crouching on the floor but thought it may be offensive. The only benefit was that she was really interested in what Lacey had to say.

"What happened that night," Mina asked?

"I had an escort appointment that had been canceled and I really needed my money," she began.

"So I went to this bar where a few interests hang out. I figured someone would want to play that night. There was this really sexy guy in the bar and he was flirting with me. It was kind of weird because he was dressed fancy. Way too fancy to be hanging out there. I still remember what he wore. A pinstriped black suit and a lavender shirt and matching tie. His shoes were black saddle shoes. He looked so…good. He must have been a professional somebody, except for that cap he wore. Tacky in my opinion. It was gray and dingy. Did not match his sexy outfit. But that's why I remember every teeny detail."

"What'd he look like, Lacey?" Mina asked.

"Never really saw his face, truthfully. He kept it covered by the cap and he also had this beard."

"Okay, so what else happened?" Mina prodded her, desperate for something more.

"When he offered me a smoke, we went outside. We talked for a second before he came on to me real strong. Now, nothing is wrong with real strong, but I need to be compensated for it. He tugged at my skirt and told me to take it off or he would. He told me that if I did what 'Daddy' asked," she said using air quotes, "I wouldn't regret it. I told him I'd give him what Daddy asked for as long as he paid for it. He didn't like that part and he backhanded me right there in the alley. Then he told me that he can make me go away and never come back. He said that he knew women like me and that I wouldn't be missed. I wasn't a lawyer or a doctor and no one would even know I was dead. That's when he smacked me so hard I hit the dumpster wall. My only saving grace was that the folks who live on top of the bar came out because of the noise. When they came out, he took off."

"Mom, can we go now?" a young voice yelled from one of the bedrooms.

"Okay, yeah, sure. Get your stuff," Lacey answered.

A cute little girl emerged with a full suitcase in tow.

"We gotta go."

"Okay, thank you for your time," Mina said, standing. "If we have questions…"

"Give me your cell phone number just in case I remember anything more," Lacey said. "You're much better than the cops here. They just assume because I'm…you know…because I like to get paid for my activities my complaints don't matter."

"Thanks again." Detective Toure stood and escorted Mina to the door.

✠✠

CHAPTER 29: DRINKS

By the time the detective returned to the precinct the next morning, he was fired up: both determined to figure out who was abusing these women and to reveal the true character of Ibra Marcus.

Toure approached Deputy Lakos's office door when he heard him slam the phone into its cradle. "No!" he shouted "No!" Hesitant to knock, the detective stood at the door for a few moments. He knocked nevertheless.

"What!" The deputy looked up with complete disdain when he saw the detective standing there. "What," he said with a growl this time.

"I thought you'd want to see me to follow up on this morning," the detective stammered and adjusted his glasses.

"Oh, I guess. Come in." Lakos seemed distracted and avoided eye contact. His cell phone rang again. This time, he stood and walked out and around the corner to answer it. As Detective Toure waited in the office, he examined his surroundings. The walls were peppered with memorabilia. Lakos's commendation awards, Hall of Fame induction, and draft pick letter hung on the wall behind his head.

Over to the side of the wall, there was a Polaroid picture was of two young boys arm in arm.

The detective scanned the desk and a scrap piece of paper caught his eye. Drawing closer, he saw that it had the address of a rundown strip mall written on it. Right under the address, someone scribbled 9:45 p.m. with today's date.

The detective looked quickly at the door and snapped a quick picture with his cell phone. After another second passed, he decided to wait elsewhere. Judging by the deputy's mood, it was best not to be there when he returned.

***

Mina picked up the phone and called Senator Kingsly. "I enjoyed last night. It was nice to get out. Are you free tonight?"

"Tonight? Sure, why not?" the senator replied, sounding intrigued.

Mina picked the restaurant and again dressed to impress. Once there, she turned on every possible charm; she was quite successful. The senator attended to her intently for the entire evening.

From the onset, Mina opted to get loose. "I'll have a vodka on the rocks."

Senator Kingsly smiled and ordered himself a cocktail. They chatted through the first round of drinks and went on to the second.

"I still wonder why I never met you before. Not at the state dinner? Not even a fundraiser?" Mina asked curiously.

"Good question. I guess things that are meant to be, are meant to be."

"Oh, you believe in fate?" Mina asked.

"I believe that we make our own. We mold it and create circumstances to fit our desired outcome," the senator said, unmoved.

"What about a higher power?" Mina asked.

"Higher than a united people with a collective voice? No," he responded.

Mina leaned in, her voice soft and sultry. "You fascinate me, Senator Kingsly. I'm really trying to get to know you. What don't I know about you? What are your likes and dislikes? Who are your friends? How do you like your job? Tell me everything!"

"Wow. That's a tall order for a quick get-together over drinks. You sound like you're trying to be the next Mrs. Kingsly." He laughed and took another long sip.

She chuckled. "Okay, maybe I'm moving super-fast. Let's start with friends."

"Us being friends?" the senator asked.

"Well, that too. But do you have friends in the Senate office?" she asked, looking at him out of the corner of her eye.

"Me?" the senator said setting his drink down. "No. I'm more of a loner type."

"Not even after these long confirmation sessions? I imagine that you receive a lot of information about the person you're confirming. Like a get-to-know-you phase. You've got to be friends with them after all that, right?"

The senator appeared to be very interested in his own thoughts. After a few seconds, he responded, "After the confirmation hearings? No, not at all. Let's take, for example, the prospective Attorney General Marcus. He and I were friends before all this, long before all this political stuff. But I tell you what, if I was just getting to know him now, the friendship would have taken a different turn."

"Oh really? Why? Isn't he likable?" Mina asked. She sipped her drink and appeared uninterested.

"No, it's not that," he retorted. "I've known him for a long time, since law school. He was a different guy back then. We've always been friends. But did you ever have a friend that you don't quite see eye to eye with anymore? It's not that you've rejected them, it's just you taken different paths in your lives."

Mina understood perfectly. Although she did not have many friends, she understood that type of separation and had used it to cut ties many times. She wanted to fully engage in this conversation, yet still she looked away, fiddled with her drink, and found a spot on the wall to avert her eyes.

"Yeah I get it," she responded, still looking away.

The senator gazed into his glass and spoke like no one was listening.

"I really wonder if people change. Or perhaps we are now allowing ourselves to be revealed."

Mina's ears perked up; she was desperate to hear more. She couldn't help it. She had to engage. "I don't know. Maybe people can change. I know I've changed over the years. The friends I grew up with wouldn't agree with my choices, my politics, my belief, my religion. I guess I've changed too."

The senator made a face, scrunching up his nose then relaxing it. "Did you change or are you truly just morphing into your true self? Maybe you— this confident beautiful self-assured person in front of me—have always been that woman. Maybe it's been covered up by layers. Maybe it's been veiled by your life choices, but maybe it's always been you." He swiveled his glass making the ice clink together.

"Maybe," Mina said distantly, taking in his words. "Is that what you think happened to your friend?"

"No, I don't think so. I think this is the person he has always been. But that's okay. To each his own, right? You do things for your friends, don't you?" he said.

"Of course," she said. She leaned into the table forcing her cleavage to show. "Now that we're friends, what are you going to do for me?"

"I thought I was doing something for you, Mrs. Blake. Do you need something more than getting to know me?" He moved in closer.

"Call me Mina. Mrs. Blake is so formal."

"Oh, I will, Mina, since we are friends now. And I expect you to call me Sam." He reached his hand out and caressed her waiting fingertips as they lay folded on the table.

She did not flinch this time nor did she pull back.

"I know it's been hard for you recently. I can only imagine your struggles and emotions right now. I would love to spend more time with you, letting you be able to lean on me. But I don't want to be too aggressive and push you away."

Mina relaxed even more. "Truthfully, Sam, I've been really lonely. I wanted to change my environment, meet someone new, and just have a good time tonight. Are you okay with that?"

The waitress arrived and informed them of the evening specials. Mina sat back comfortably, her legs crossed and shoulders loose.

"How long have you been in the Senate, Sam?"

"At this point, it's been eight or nine years now," he replied.

"What are your confirmation hearings like? It sounds so exciting," she said, feigning interest.

"They're really not. We get information. We weigh in among our party, and then as a conglomerate, we vote on it. Nothing too interesting. Trust me," he said dryly.

"Oh really? That's strange to me. My husband was really into the back story for folks. Seems like he put together a really great back story on a few of the candidates."

"That would make sense to me. That was the responsibility of the team that he was heading up," Sam said.

He beckoned for the waitress and ordered additional drinks for them.

"Really?" Mina continued. "Don't you think there's something strange about getting so much information about a person before the confirmation hearing?"

"No, not at all. That's pretty standard. With Oren especially. I think he took pleasure in that part. You never really find too much anyhow. We have a private investigator and our background checks are initially run by our police department. They should turn everything up for us and hand it right on over. By the time we vote, it is a simple formality."

Mina straightened up. "Really, so everything is uncovered by the police department first?"

"For sure. That process is pretty thorough. It goes through their leadership for approval and then is sent our way. Interestingly enough, they've never uncovered a questionable past with anyone," Sam said, before gulping the last of his drink.

"No one?" Mina pushed.

"Nope. No one," he countered. "But that's enough talk about my job. Let's talk about you."

The food arrived but Mina was barely able to eat. The spread was delectable. The pasta was al dente, just as she liked it. The sauces were creamy and the seafood was delightfully cooked to perfection. Despite her favorite foods and a truly enjoyable environment, Mina moved her food from one side of the plate to the other. She'd had quite a few vodkas by that time and had forgotten how quickly alcohol affected her. Her head was spinning but she tried hard to focus. She tried to replay the entire conversation in her head so as not to miss a thing. Suddenly, she dropped her fork with a clang in the middle of her plate, drawing the attention of other diners to her.

"What's the matter, Mina? Don't like yours?" the senator asked with a mouth full of sauce.

"Here, taste mine." He offered her a forkful from his plate.

Mina the shook her head "No" slowly.

"Full from the appetizers, I'll bet," the senator added.

"It must be the drinks," Mina said.

"Let's get out of here," he suggested. "We can wrap that up and take it with us. How about my place? We can hang out a little longer. Maybe your appetite will return." Sam stood and stroked Mina's locks as he spoke.

She looked up at him, disturbed that she enjoyed the feeling of his hands in her hair.

"I don't think I've told you this tonight, Mina, but your eyes are mesmerizing. You truly look like you are seeing through me. I desire to share my entire self with you, especially when you gaze at me like that."

Appreciative of the compliment but certain that she could not trust him, Mina mumbled a disingenuous, "Thank you."

The senator arranged for the food to be packed up. He led her out of the restaurant and into the waiting car. She sat on the passenger side and took every opportunity to lean against the door, silently begging it to hold her body up.

"Aww, not yet," Sam pleaded. "Don't fall asleep yet, Mina. Our evening is just beginning." He nudged her lightly.

Mina tried but continued to fade. Once she opened her eyes they were at the entrance of a gated community. The rambling homes were elaborate and expensive. The townhouses seemed so modest in comparison. The senator pulled into a driveway where a black Porsche was parked. That car's license plate read: KINGS. Entering a code on his cell phone, the garage door opened.

"This is my home, Mina. Please make yourself comfortable. I'll be right back."

He walked her to the living room and slipped to a back room. Her eyes were so tired she did not even attempt to follow him with her gaze. The senator returned in moments with a glass of bubbly liquid.

"Drink this. It will make you feel better."

"What is it?" she protested.

"Don't worry about it. Daddy will take good care of you," he responded.

He sat down beside her and put the glass to her lips.

"Drink it," he said sternly. As he intently held the glass to Mina's lips, the noise of his cell phone alarm startled them both.

"What the—" He put the cup down and grabbed his phone. "Hell. We gotta go."

He helped Mina up forcibly and quickly led her to his car in the garage. "We'll have to continue this another time. I forgot I have an appointment tonight."

They headed to the capitol building. By this time Mina started to get a little more lucid.

"This is where I leave you, sweet goddess. How about tomorrow? Shall we continue?" he asked.

Mina stood, unsteadily getting out of his car. "Give me a call," she said holding her head.

Without hesitation, the senator peeled out of the parking lot and disappeared down the street.

✣✣
CHAPTER 30: 9:45

Detective Toure considered the possibility of showing up at the abandoned market all evening. He vacillated to the point of annoying himself. He even debated calling Officer Snow to accompany him but thought better of it. He thought about calling Candace to investigate with him but he remembered with painful clarity how useless she was at the last event.

While thinking about Candace, a pang of anxiety hit him. Detective Toure found Candace uniquely exquisite. He thought she had taken an interest in him as well. He assumed that the outfit she chose was clearly intended for him.

How could I think otherwise? he pondered. *And that hug. The date began with us locked in an embrace. She was definitely interested in me.*

Detective Toure continued to torture himself with those thoughts.

Maybe soon, he fantasized. *But as for tonight, Candace cannot help me.*

He picked up the phone to call Mina. Even though they hadn't known each other long, Detective Toure trusted her. It rang a few times and went straight to voice mail. He hung up and texted her:

HEADED OUT TONIGHT. CASE RELATED. COME.

He figured the text, although cryptic, would be explanatory. When Mina saw it, she would either call or text and that would be that. But he received no call or text. Determined not to miss this opportunity, Detective Toure opted to go alone. He only knew how to get there and where to go. Nothing else. There was a great possibility that the detective was walking into an orchestrated trap. Nevertheless, he put on some grubby jeans and an old lumber jacket and jumped into his car.

The ride to the shopping center was more tiresome than he remembered. It was far, and the darkness amplified his impatience. The road was dark and winding. The wind howled and whipped his small car to and fro. During the drive, the detective contemplated his position. He could bust in Dirty Harry style, or sneak in like 007. He entertained himself with these thoughts but still didn't have a plan. Despite his true desire to emerge as a hero, it wasn't going to happen like that. By the time he arrived, he was intent on staying hidden but close enough to hear and hopefully see.

He approached the vacant strip mall and saw three vehicles parked outside a detached market; the cars were dark and uninhabited. Nevertheless, the detective felt his heart racing a bit as the reality of his personal stakeout started to hit him. The market was dimly lit and confined to a small area.

Fighting the urge to turn back and retreat to his comfortable apartment, he pulled up alongside the cars and turned off his headlights as he approached. When his fear hit a crescendo, he opted not to stop there. Across the street, there was a field overgrown with bramble. It was the perfect place to remain hidden, so he pulled in and camouflaged himself and his car for the moment.

As he sat in his car, Detective Toure breathed heavily. His heart was racing to the point that he was nearly hyperventilating. He was petrified at the thought of getting out of the car but could not justify any reason for staying inside. With shaky hands, he opened his car door, certain he was drawing too much attention to himself. Looking to the left and to the right, he realized there were no other inhabitants for many feet. The market was in the center of a clearing with not much of anything surrounding it. Crouching down low and trying to recall all tactics that he learned as a young officer, he maneuvered across the street.

Three cars were parked haphazardly in the parking lot. The detective did not recognize any of them. Not wanting to waste precious undetected time, he had only one choice. The market had a long wall of floor-to-ceiling windows. They were covered with shades that attempted to block out intruding eyes. Detective Toure was instantly dismayed when he saw that there were relatively no hiding places on the outside of the building. He would either have to get close enough to watch what was going on or find his way to the inside. Judging by the individuals he thought were inside, the detective did not want to join them. No covert mission that he considered himself skilled enough to execute could get him inside.

Perplexed, he wondered how he would gain info and intel on the outside of this pivotal meeting. The market was still masked in darkness. As Detective Toure drew closer, he saw a very dim light coming from the front left of the building. He was careful not to get close, even to the windows.

He turned on his cell phone for the small stream of light that it provided. Shining it against the faded brick, the detective saw a unit that once had an industrial air conditioner. He passed on the option of climbing into it and possibly unearthing things that would be best left undisturbed. Again, faced with no other alternatives, Detective Toure checked the rear of the building, taking careful steps. He flinched at each step, scared that he would either see a cornered animal prepared to strike or the remnants of a dead one. Detective Toure was not prepared to see either.

He drew his weapon as he walked and continued a prayer mantra in his head.

Around back, he discovered a conglomerate of broken beer bottles, old tires, and evidence of used drug paraphernalia. He was relieved it was nothing more. The hard ground crunched under his feet, and all sorts of debris crumbled under his boots. With each sound, the voice in his head urged him to turn around, but he didn't. He maintained the light from his cell phone and kept crouching until he found the rear air conditioning unit. He eyed the building and judged that lit area was a mere thirty feet away. He turned off his cell phone and relied on the nearly nonexistent street lights. He was completely against the idea of climbing into the air conditioner opening but saw no other options. Desperate, he spied the area for other entrances into the building. Out of the corner of his eye, he detected a small window with a broken glass pane.

This window differed from the wall of windows on the other side of the building. Peering in before taking any action, Detective Toure found that it led to a small room. It was likely the manager's office in the market. It did not take much to push the window open. As he hoisted it up, Detective Toure heard raised voices. He wasn't sure if they were arguing or just loud talkers. The detective was able to climb through the window and land quietly in the open space of the office. He made virtually no noise and breathed quietly. He was set on getting in and out undetected.

From where he was positioned, the detective could see absolutely nothing but could hear pretty clearly. Although slightly muffled, the conversation was audible. It was evident that there were three men speaking, each with different intonations and pitches.

"Listen, man, it's all on you now," one said.

"Are you proceeding with the plans?" asked another.

"I'm not sure about all this," said a third.

"We agreed!" the first voice yelled.

"We never agreed, and I'm not sure this is a good idea," the third voice responded as angrily.

"Are you using the drugs?" the second voice asked.

"Yeah, why are we even using that?" the first voice asked.

"Look, fellas, I got us a hookup! Use the drugs I gave you!" the second voice commanded.

"Either you're all in or we're all out. It's as simple as that. What's your choice?" the first voice queried the group.

"But why do we have to use this? Why can't we just do it on our own?" the third voice protested.

"Listen. We are all getting them and getting that high. Trust me—there is nothing more intoxicating than feeling that high," the second voice urged.

"So?" the first voice continued. "We're all in."

"Of course," the second voice chimed. "I'll be doing it too. You have the stuff?"

There was a pause and some shuffling.

"So, we'll check back in a week?" the first voice said. "You better have something to tell me. Don't force my hand."

The third man's voice was now quivering. "Force your hand? What do you mean by that? Nothing," he responded "Right?"

"Right," the second voice responded.

"I'm leaving," the third voice said.

"Don't forget five days. Right here at nine forty-five," the first voice said.

"I won't," the third voice mumbled.

The third man walked heavily across the floor, which squeaked under his feet. He went out through a front door that slammed behind him.

The other two men continued talking.

"What's the status? I'm not convinced that I want another one like the last one," the first voice said.

"This is a game changer, man. We can go either way with this. No one can say 'No.'" The second voice said emphatically.

The detective heard all he needed to hear. Slipping back through the window, he replaced it silently. No longer concerned about animals living and dead, paraphernalia or debris, the detective ran at high speed from the rear of the market along the periphery to his car. Once safely in his car, he continued to breathe heavily. His hands shook so intensely he had trouble gripping the steering wheel. Despite that, he managed to start the ignition and slowly pull away, drawing no attention.

✠

CHAPTER 31: TRANSFORMED

The following afternoon, Senator Kingsly sent a half a dozen long-stemmed roses to Mina's home. They were so elegant and it had been so long since Mina received attention like this, that she was a little flattered. She couldn't even figure out what to do with them. Candace took over in the domestic area as she often did and made a prominent home for the bouquet in the front room. It was evident more than ever that the senator was interested. Mina was interested in him too, but not for the reasons he'd have expected. She resolved to continue to make herself accessible to him. She wasn't sure how far as she was willing to go, but there was no off button in sight.

Right after sending a brief thank-you text, she received a curt response. It simply said, "TONIGHT AT MY PLACE?"

Mina responded, "YES. WHEN?"

"7:30"

She was determined not to miss any opportunity to corner the senator. That evening, she dressed more casually: a form-fitting pair of jeans, a black tee, and a bright pink blazer. Casual for her did not mean that she omitted her pink stilettos. Pleased with her look, she headed out.

Senator Kingsly met her at the door. "Ravishing, as usual, Mina."

Mina smiled and opened her arms for a hug. "Nice to see you tonight, Senator," she joked.

"Mrs. Blake, the pleasure is all mine." He smiled back.

"Tell me, Sam, what's on the agenda tonight. I couldn't wait to come over."

"Well, Mina, the menu is fabulous, the entertainment is top notch, and the company will make you want to come back for more."

Mina cozied into the evening laughing and joking with Sam. She had a great time…without any alcohol no less. *Not tonight*, she vowed.

Sam made himself a few drinks; he consumed them while he cooked.

"What can I get you, Mina? Red or white," he asked.

"Neither thanks," she replied.

"Are you sure?"

"I'm certain tonight," she said.

"Okay then. What other type of beverage would you desire?" the senator asked politely.

"I'll just take a glass of whatever soda you have on tap, for now, thanks."

Sam handed her a glass. After taking three sips, she started to feel lightheaded.

"Can I lie on your couch?" she asked, her voice feeble.

"Of course you can, Mina. Do you feel all right?"

"Yeah, I'm sure I'll be fine. I just need to rest for a moment."

The senator guided her to the couch and helped her lie down. He lifted her legs and helped her stretch out. In moments, she drifted off into a comfortable sleep, but true to form, she woke up every couple of minutes. She hadn't been able to sleep soundly since Oren's death. This evening was no exception, despite her wooziness.

When she opened her eyes the last time, she found the senator six inches away from her with his pants unzipped and down by his thighs.

"Sam!" she yelled.

She sat up but immediately fell back down. Her body was heavy and immobile. The entire weight of her struggle kept her affixed to the couch. Her muscles yearned to move and be active, but to no avail. All she was able to do was elevate her consciousness. Her body was trapped but her mind was free. She felt a breeze on her face, a tightening in her belly, and a warmth that overtook her. The heat that she emitted was beautifully controlled and systematic.

"Eshu," she whispered and was lifted, feeling a sense of consciousness and his essence.

In that moment, Mina was pulled out of her present circumstance and transported above her own body. She hovered in observation. She felt free and able to tap into the ability to enjoy her new nature. Equipped with a feeling of flight, Mina could have taken herself anywhere. She visualized the peacefulness of water and the calming effect of the waves. She considered going right back to the tranquility of Jamaica. She looked down at her body trapped in the circumstance that her mind had escaped. She saw Sam hovering over her with his pants unzipped and hands in them. She saw the desire in his eyes but not for pleasure or enjoyment but for domination. She felt his energy and read his intentions. Mina felt his hatred and perversion as he fondled himself. With one hand he stroked Mina's long locks, wrapping her hair around his exposed body.

Mina's peace and calm faded fast. The fire in her belly intensified. She heard the drums. As they grew louder she heard the chanting. It was not just one, but it was a chorus: the chanting of a group. Mina was not alone; she was supported on either side. As far as her essence could determine, she was accompanied.

The chanting grew louder and was interrupted by a blood-curdling high-pitched yell. The war had begun, and Mina was at the head. She felt herself being outfitted. Her muscles tightened and contracted as she transformed into the warrior she'd suppressed until now. As Mina changed, the fire in her belly consumed her fear. She initiated the scream that began the fight. She jumped back into her lying body with a vengeance. The tiredness, fatigue, and effects of whatever she ingested dissipated immediately.

Mina leaped off the couch quickly and with precision. She grabbed the wineglass Sam had given her. Remnants of the substance that tried to desecrate her temple remained in the glass. Mina slammed the glass on the coffee table and watched it shatter, letting the last of the liquid spill to the carpet. The glass stem and jagged pieces made for a very effective weapon.

In one swift leap, Mina jumped onto the table like a puma. She yoked Sam's neck with her left hand, choking him, poised to squeeze his very life and crush his windpipe. Her thumb hung over his Adam's apple and her right hand wielded her weapon, aimed at his exposed manhood.

"I will castrate you and cut off your air supply in three seconds. I suggest you don't move." Mina spoke with guttural grit.

Her eyes narrowed and her newly hazel eyes were now black. The drums beat loudly. She was not the beauty the senator had invited into his home. She was a threat and was in complete control of this moment. Mina pushed her weapon steadily to meet Sam's flesh. He let out a yelp.

"Mina—please, no!" he pleaded.

She gripped his neck more tightly and he gasped for air.

"Mina—please don't!"

"I will *never* be your slave!" she screamed.

A bead of blood started to form at the site of the weapon.

Sam grunted.

Mina pulled back, changing her aim. She was now intent on thrusting her jagged glass spear swiftly through his chest. She intending to break the skin, penetrate the muscles, and sever blood vessels. The drums became louder, vibrating through her entire body. Sam's death was imminent. Mina knew exactly where she needed to aim and slowly brought her weapon there.

As she prepared to strike, the drums ceased abruptly and the waves began. She heard the crashing of the waves and smelled the salt water. She saw the foam lifting and carrying itself to shore. Mina was no longer in Sam's living room but on the shores of her homeland. She was barefoot and dressed in white. She did not feel alone but she was surrounded by the peace that enveloped her. There was not a single body around her, and she reveled in the blues and the whites: blue sky, white waves, blue sea, white sand.

She saw the caretaking and the caring of her people and felt the individual energy of every inhabitant on the earth. It filled her soul and she swelled. She felt life happening and exploding into existence right before her eyes. Birthing and labor pains overtook her as waves. As her consciousness traveled, Mama Blake appeared on the shores with her.

"Woye! Yes, mi dear! Whatcha!" Mama Blake embraced Mina with the unconditional love of a mother. They swayed together to the sound of the waves.

"Ya strong, ya hear!" Mama Blake said in her ears.

Mina cried and hugged Mama Blake longer. Mama Blake passed through her arms and retreated into the waters.

As Mama Blake became the waters, a light wind whipped around Mina. It rose from the waves and grew stronger—more powerful and more distinct. The wind formed the outline of a woman; it mixed with the seas and became a tangible person.

Mina didn't know who she was, but she felt her greatness and fell to her knees.

"Great Mother," she said reverently with her head held low.

"I am called Yemaya," the presence stated.

"Yes," Mina responded. "Why have you come?

"I come to those who seek me, love."

"With all due reverence, I didn't seek you," Mina said with her head still held low.

Yemaya smiled and lifted Mina from her knees. "Your life sought me. I am your stillness, your water. You've sought me for a long time. I needed you to know I'm here."

Mina breathed in the smell of the life-giving water. She closed her eyes and felt the air on her face. She felt her feet grounded in the sand. As the air became cooler, she felt her arms and the objects that were in her hands. She felt the coldness of death in her right hand. Letting go moments before impact, she dropped the glass. The additional millisecond would have witnessed the collision of the glass and

Sam's chest. The broken wineglass shattered when it fell. Mina slowly released her grip from around Sam's neck.

With a clean Capoeira technique, she lifted her leg and landed a swift kick into his chest. She moved into a roundhouse and caught him on the side of his cheek with another kick.

He doubled over and gasped for air.

"Oh my God, oh my God," he continued to repeat.

Enraged, Mina leaped and landed on his chest, punching him swiftly in the jaw. "It *was* the gods. And pull up your pants!" she growled.

Sam appeared to take her words seriously.

"Lie down and don't move," she ordered still straddling his chest.

Mina reached for her phone.

"Detective, we have an emergency. I need you to get here right now. And bring Candace with you."

***

Detective Toure sat in the Sam's living room alongside Candace. Senator Sam Kingsly sat squirming in handcuffs, his face bloody.

Sam was sweating profusely, his breaths coming in short bursts. Yet Mina was stern-faced and aggressive. She was intimidating and the darkness she experienced was still close to the surface. She sat back, drinking a bottled water and staring intently at the man across from her.

Detective Toure walked toward Sam, folded his arms, and stood wide legged. "You better start talking. I don't need to remind you of how fickle your constituents are. I'm going to ruin you. But the question is, am I going to ruin you and send you to prison to be raped by men, or am I going to ruin you and leave you in financial ruin for the rest of your life, disgraced and destitute. Choose your poison, Senator."

Senator Kingsly broke down into whimpers and wails. Mucus ran down his nose and into his mouth. He wiped his nose with his expensive, monogrammed shirtsleeves.

"Don't do this," he pleaded. "I can tell you everything. We can strike a deal."

The senator continued looking distraught and now wrung his hands while still in handcuffs.

The detective began, "You see, this lovely woman can choose to press charges for assault and attempted rape and that is the end. Every judge in this country and every jury in this world will see fit to put you underneath the jail. And so ends your career, your life, your reputation. Poof! It's all gone. But by the same token, this lovely specimen of God's grace may see fit to not press charges. Thereby, you get your life back. But given that you believe it's all right to drug women and take advantage of a narcotic-induced stupor, I'm betting she's going to throw the book at you."

Sam shot Mina a pleading look. "Mina—"

"Mrs. Blake," she corrected.

"Mrs. Blake, I can help you. I can tell you anything you want to know. I'm a wealth of information," Sam begged.

"Do you think I will trust you? Mina yelled. "To even do something simple like tell the truth? You are filth." She looked directly into his eyes. "I'm done here, Detective. Take his ass outta here," she said dismissively, waving her hand.

"I can help you, Mina. I mean Mrs. Blake." A few tears escaped from his eyes and rolled down his cheek.

The detective tapped Mina on the shoulder and backed her into a corner. Candace wandered over to join the huddle. "Mina, I know he is a jerk. And he would have raped you if you didn't kick his ass. But I also know that he is too dumb to do this alone. We can get more information from him if he's working for us. Actually, not with us—for us."

Candace looked at Mina, her eyes warm and sympathetic. "Mina, he is right. This guy couldn't do it alone. You see how he is blubbering over there? That's not the look of the kingpin. How much you want to bet he's tied to that other jerk."

Mina nodded her head. "Yeah, I suppose so. So, where do we go from here?"

Detective Toure interjected, placing his hand on both of the women's shoulders. "I'll take it from here. Mina, get in your Capoeira stance just in case you have to spring into action again."

"Looks like we're back in business," Candace said.

"And—don't fall for the enemy this time," Mina said looking at Candace disapprovingly.

Detective Toure returned to Sam who still sat on the couch.

"This is what we want, Senator. You are going to spend the next few hours telling us everything you know about this drug and the folks you are in cahoots with. After tonight, we will check in daily and you will continue to assist us with information about what led to the murder of Oren Blake.

"Murder! I don't know anything about a murder!" the senator yelled.

"Let us be the judge of that," Detective Toure replied calmly. "Do we have a deal?"

"What do I get out of it?" Sam asked.

"First of all, you're lucky not to be sitting in lockup right now." Detective Toure raised his voice. "I believe we can request the benevolence of Mrs. Blake to not press charges. But it's up to her. Like I said, do we have a deal?"

"Yeah," the senator mumbled. "Yeah, we do."

Mina walked over and whispered in the senator's ear. "If you so much as touch me, brush up against me in a crowded room, mistakenly reach for the doorknob when I do—if the skin on my arm comes in any contact with the skin on yours—I *will* kill you." Her voice dripped with quiet and controlled rage.

The senator bit his lip and seemed to try to control himself.

The detective uncuffed him and Candace put a bottle of water in front of him on the table. He wrung his wrists and stretched out his fingers.

"Give me your phone, Senator," Detective Toure demanded.

"My phone? Why?"

"Simple insurance. You won't call or text anyone until we have what we need."

"You guys think I'm crazy!" the senator said turning over his phone.

The detective placed it on the counter out of arm's reach.

"I'm already going to be in a boatload of hot water if they're on to me," he whined. "Look, for me to do this I still have to protect myself. I have an idea. I can tell you, but better still—I can make sure that they tell you. Take me out of the mix and let them be responsible for their part in this!"

"What are you saying, Senator?" The detective got in Sam's face.

"I'm just saying, my word is one thing, but wouldn't you prefer to hear the word from those really behind this?"

"Are you on our side?" Mina asked.

"I'm covering *my* side, Mrs. Blake," the senator pleaded.

"That's good enough for me," Candace said.

"Start talking," the detective demanded again.

"Okay. Let me start with the fact that I am so very sorry, Mrs. Blake. I've never ever done anything like this before and thank God I didn't do it today." His eyes darted from Mina to Candace to the detective. "There is an experimental drug that has just hit the streets. The guys that I'm friends with know it all too well. They wanted me to test it out and see if its effects on women are the same as an intense high. I'm told that one pill dissolved in any kind of drink will make you feel subservient and very agreeable. Not only will it mellow you out, but it should put you in a stupor to the point that your body can't put up a fight—it inhibits the fight-or-flight response in the brain. I will admit that continual use produces irreversible psychosis. Abusers can expect everything that comes with complete psychosis. It'll get you high, then make you crazy." Sam paused lowering his head.

"My part in this was to test it on one person and see how effective it was. I don't get out much. And because of my reputation, I would never be caught dead soliciting a prostitute or anything." The senator looked up sheepishly. "The timing with Mrs. Blake was impeccable. Plus, she asked me out."

Candace shot Mina a hateful look.

Mina averted her eyes and stared angrily at the senator.

Sam kept talking. "If Mrs. Blake didn't seem like she was interested, then I would have had no opportunity anyway. But she seemed interested and I had this pill that I needed to test out."

Appearing sincere, he looked at Mina. "Thank you for saving me tonight, Mrs. Blake. I'm not that kind of man. And for the record, I really enjoyed your company."

"Shut the—" Mina said, popping him in the mouth.

Candace shook her head and handed the senator a paper towel for his bloody lip.

"So, how did you get hooked up with this experimental drug anyway?" Candace asked. "What kind of friends do you have?"

The senator paused and took a swig of his water. Pursing his lips and nodding his head he let out a deep sigh. "I know you guys owe me nothing but I can't have this come back to me."

"What on earth are you talking about?" Candace asked, grimacing. "Just spit it out."

The senator paused, obviously choosing his words carefully. "My friends are in high places. Mrs. Blake, we spoke of this before. I have friends and I don't always approve of their activities. Some, I choose to turn a blind eye to. All that I've been told is that this drug is going to revolutionize the way men maintain the upper hand when the situation calls for it."

"Um, does that sound like rape to you?" Mina mused. "It does to me."

The senator nodded. "I guess it does, but I never thought they'd actually do that."

"Who is this *they* that you speak of?" the detective asked.

"Oh, did I not say?" the senator spoke, looking smug.

"It's Ibra Marcus, isn't it?" Candace asked.

"And Deputy Lakos," the detective said.

The senator nodded his head. "It is," he responded matter-of-factly.

"Who else?" Mina demanded. "Who else is in this perverted ring?"

"No one else, Mrs. Blake. Believe me," Sam pleaded. "And it's not a ring. I've known these guys for twenty years. I'd always heard that Ibra and the deputy were into some unique stuff. But I figured it was all rumors. You know, when people are jealous of you, they spread rumors. And Ibra and the deputy were the ones to watch. They've always been."

The senator pined a little bit as he spoke.

"They just shared this drug with me last week or so. Before that, we would just get together or hang out and have a good time. No crazy stuff." The senator flailed his arms wildly as he spoke. "Oh my God! I just can't believe this!" He put his head in his hands. "It's all starting to make sense, though. You guys might want to settle in—it's going to be a long night."

✠✠

CHAPTER 32: SAM'S TALE

"I've known Ibra since we were students at law school. He introduced me to his best friend. His brother, he called him: Steven Lakos. They were both jocks. Steven had made it big in the NBA but suffered an injury. That's where I come in. Ibra went to be by his brother's side and basically left school. But we had just become friends so I gave him my notes, my outlines, my case studies. Whatever I knew, he knew. He passed his 2L year because of me." Kingsly smirked. "The crazy thing is that he'll admit it too. Our third year, right at the cusp of becoming professionals, me and Ibra moved in together. We'd study hard and play even harder. But that was when I started to hear rumors. Steven was now in rehab with no job and no career, so he had nothing but time on his hands. He'd come see us regularly. Together, the three of us were the life of the party."

Sam paused, as if gathering his thoughts. He asked for some water and Detective Toure handed him a glass.

"There was this one time, we had the party of the year. There were girls, booze, weed, barbiturates, music. Everything you could think of—and it was a good time. When I say good time, trust me. I haven't always been this buttoned up. The next morning, after the party was over, there were like bodies everywhere. Folks were still hungover and weren't talking straight. One of the 1Ls was looking for her roommate who'd come to the party with her. Considering everything that happened, no one was really concerned about her missing friend. They figured she hooked up with some guy and left. But her roommate was adamant that she was with Ibra the last time she saw her. She said Ibra was all over her and they went outside to do...whatever. Again, because the environment was wild, anything could've happened with anyone." Sam took a sip of his water.

"The thing is," he said after swallowing, "I remember seeing that 1L girl with Ibra too, but Steven convinced me it wasn't Ibra—that it was some other dude. I was real messed up by that time so I dismissed it. A few weeks later, I heard that the girl wasn't in school anymore. Her roommate insisted that she wasn't seen after our party, but somehow the story came out that she dropped out and went home. That never sat well with me." He furrowed his brow as if the grim reality was only now starting to sink in, before he continued. "One of the evening students worked as a police officer during the day. He used to tell me what he considered isolated cases. There had been reports of missing women that took our small college town by storm. Remember, the law school is about two hours from here. There's no big-city action down that way."

"But you said isolated, just now," Mina asked.

"According to my friend, they were," Sam continued. "It seemed that there was a different MO for each incident. There was no consistency among the missing in terms of age, educational background, physical attributes. And in one instance, a man was among the missing."

"So wait a second," Candace interjected. "Considering what we know now, is it possible Ibra was just getting started? Based on Oren's work, this would be the first time that the missing or attacks were outside of a school."

"Oren?" asked the senator. "What did Oren have to do with all of this?"

Mina shared the findings with Sam. She spoke in painstaking detail and unearthed all of the documentation that Oren maintained.

"Holy Moses! Are you kidding me?" Sam slunk back into his chair and rubbed his temples. "Can you access everything that you're telling me about?"

"Everything," Mina confirmed touching the pendant that hung around her neck.

"My cop friend used to tell me of the ongoing assaults that happened that year," Sam continued. "It seemed that out of all of his years on the force, our third year was particularly active. He always used to joke and say that the criminals knew we were almost attorneys and were preparing the way for us."

Sam stared at the wall as he spoke barely above a whisper. "Geesh, do you think Ibra is really capable of all this?"

"You tell me, Senator," the detective said. "You actually know this man. What else do you know, Senator? Seems like he is not the saint you thought he was."

Sam's voice was harsh and insistent. "I don't know what Ibra and Steven are into. We're friends but not like that. I do know about our outings, though." His voice softened. "I can tell you about the women."

"Whenever we met up out of town, it was always a little bit off. I mean, the guys would regularly take off for a few hours leaving me with a slew of women. Ibra and Steven always had women waiting in the wings for us. I think I do all right with the women, and I've never had a problem picking up a hot chick—especially not in the places where we hung out. But for whatever reason, there were always at least two ladies chatting it up with me, keeping me company, keeping me occupied while the guys were gone. They were generally well spoken, seemingly smart, but like falling-down drunk. A few times, I got up to leave with the guys, but Steven always said that I had to hold it down for them. Now, the women were always sloppy by this time. I really used to wonder how I was always with the high ones…" His voice trailed off.

"But I still don't get it. They just told me about this new thing that they wanted to try out. Just. That doesn't make sense to me. You mean they had already been using it successfully?"

Mina looked at the senator disapprovingly and shook her head. "Maybe successful isn't the right word."

"Sorry! I'm at a complete loss here!" Sam yelled, exasperated. He covered his face with his hands.

Detective Toure sat on the floor. "If I didn't know better, I'd say this experimental drug has been used a few times before. Sounds like we're on the cusp of a larger distribution circle," he said.

Sam stared off, emotionless for a minute or two.

Candace had made her way into his kitchen. She returned with mugs, a teapot, a box of crackers, and a tin of mixed nuts.

Sam peeked at her from the gaps between his fingers.

"You said for us to settle in," she said.

Mina made her tea and spoke carefully. "I think I understand it all now. Sam, how many other folks were given this drug with you?"

"I think it was just me. They never mentioned anyone else. When we met about it, it was only us."

"And Ibra's confirmation hearing? Who else runs that show?" Mina asked.

"I'm the chair. There's really no opposition," Sam stated. "It's practically a done deal. Our sources didn't uncover the information that Oren unearthed."

"Hmmm," Mina mused and sat up authoritatively. "What do you guys think of this?"

She spoke intently, punctuating each word. "We are going to bring them down. All of us. Including you, Senator."

The detective nodded and sat on his heels. The senator looked at Mina quizzically. And Candace grinned from ear to ear and placed her mug down on the counter.

✠✠

CHAPTER 33: RESEARCH

Detective Toure didn't get much sleep that night. By the time they left Sam's apartment, it was well after 3:00 a.m. Toure tossed and turned during the night, disappointed and surprisingly filled with fear. After all these years on the force, he still considered himself a mediocre detective. He thought about how he'd gained great publicity last year taking down the middleman of a small theft ring. That feat got him promoted to detective. He was proud of his accomplishments but wasn't sure that he was ready for this. He was good at being consistent. His family chided him on a regular basis for his great ability to be either black or white. If he liked someone, he let them know and if he didn't, he let them know that as well. When it came to Detective Toure, there were absolutely no mixed messages—he was a no-nonsense kind of man. The next few days were going to be a challenge. He felt it and he was scared.

The following morning, despite his fatigue, Detective Toure was up and out early. He didn't know what he was going to do, but he was determined to act with intention when dealing with Deputy Lakos. He sat outside the deputy's office and waited on the bench like a schoolboy. He was nervous, as though it were the first day of school.

Deputy Lakos sauntered in wearing sunglasses. Although the office caught a great deal of sunlight, it did not warrant shades.

"Is everything okay this morning, Deputy?" Detective Toure asked, trying his best to sound exceptionally chipper.

"I'm fine," was all Lakos said.

"I grabbed us some coffees. Figured we could use it. Jumping right back in the Martin case, right?" Detective Toure quipped.

The deputy accepted the coffee and mumbled thanks.

"Yeah sure," he said. "Just give me a minute to get myself together." He started to close the door.

"I'll wait in your office then," the detective said, pushing the slightly closed door back open.

At this point, Lakos did not seem to be paying any attention to Detective Toure. He sat behind his large desk and fiddled with his phone.

"I've been checking out her file," Detective Toure started talking, very aware of the tension in the room. He moved into his habit of rambling, which he often did when nervous. "She was last seen leaving her job. That seems to be really consistent. These women were either at their places of employment or something job related. Don't you find that curious? I do. I was thinking that we should go by her job today."

The detective's ramblings must have started to annoy Lakos. The deputy rolled his eyes and swore under his breath.

"We've already done that," Lakos retorted quickly. "The investigation team went there weeks ago."

Unabashed, the detective carried on. "True, but according to the file, her boss was out of town. I don't see a statement from her. It couldn't hurt." Toure remained as cool as he could, considering that his voice was quivering. "I'm ready when you are."

The deputy grabbed his keys off the desk. "Come on," he ordered.

By the time the interviews were done, Deputy Lakos looked about ready to explode. Detective Toure called for interviews with the boss, the supervisor, and a very close workmate. He asked every question he could think of: something right out of the textbooks. He was also careful to record the details of their answers. He obtained more background information than was in the file and was pleased to share that information on their drive back. Proud of himself, the detective chatted incessantly in the car.

They pulled up to the precinct again having been gone for about two hours. As quickly as he was able to turn off the engine, the deputy climbed out and left the detective seated right there. By the time Detective Toure left the car, Lakos was nowhere to be found. Despite that, Detective Toure went back to his office ready to keep working the case. The door was ajar but the office was empty.

"Deputy Lakos," he called.

The detective pushed the door open and stepped inside. There was a file on the left corner of the desk. The only reason he noticed it was because it was in a dark blue folder with the writing: CLOSED CASE. He lifted it and examined the outside of the file. It had the usual markings: case name, open date, disposition, and closed date. The file was the *People vs Johannes Maximillian*. On quick perusal, he learned that Johannes was implicated and indicted on several counts of drug dealing, production, and sales. The detective read on. The summary indicated that the drug was more addictive than cocaine, highly concentrated, and potentially lethal.

As he stood, Detective Toure heard people speaking outside the room. His heart started to beat quickly as he realized what would happen if he was caught reading the file.

"Oh, Deputy! Quick question for you." It seemed one of the officers had stopped the deputy and was speaking loudly in the hallway.

The detective shoved the papers back into the file and tried to organize them the way he'd found them.

"We done here?" he heard the deputy respond.

Detective Toure's hands shook as he replaced the file on the left side of the desk. He moved quickly to the door, which was still slightly open. His heart reverberated in his chest. He slipped out the office, careful not to widen the door opening, and slid his body to the bench outside.

"Detective. Again?" the deputy sounded exasperated and addressed him dryly. "I have a few things to attend to outside of this case. I *am* the deputy—soon to be chief of the department, you know."

Detective Toure scrambled to his feet, heart still beating hard and fast.

"No problem," he said. "We can continue tomorrow morning."

Detective Toure left before the deputy was able to say anything more. He immediately went to his desk and wrote down the name he'd seen so it would not escape him afterward. Johannes Maximilian. He was not familiar with that name but was going to find out. Detective Toure started to look up names on old case files. He checked the internal system against the name and turned up a case blurb and the disposition.

When he selected the file to get more information, he received an error message.

"Locked?" he said out loud. "Why would we lock a case?"

A few of his colleagues lifted their heads and looked in Detective Toure's direction as he realized he was being exceptionally loud.

"Sorry," he whispered and went back to his computer.

The blurb did not give much more information. It reiterated what was on the outside of the blue folder along with another sentence or two. The case disposition stated that the charges were withdrawn. Johannes was released with no additional charges pending. The detective did not understand. Cases of this caliber were generally charged, prosecuted heavily, and most times, the individual received a prison sentence of some kind.

"I don't get it!" the detective said more softly this time.

Determined to get answers, he called a friend at the state department. Without giving his source any additional background information, Detective Toure asked for help.

"Yeah sure. No problem, Detective. How's my sister doing?"

"She's doing great. She just helped me on a case last week," the detective responded. "In any case, I really appreciate this."

"Of course. I was able to pull it up and I'll just e-mail it to you."

"Umm, if you don't mind, can you stick it in the mail instead?"

"You'll have it in hand tomorrow."

"You are the best. I'll tell Snow I talked to you."

He hung up feeling accomplished. Now all that was left was to dig up a little information on Deputy Steven Lakos. There was obviously much more to him than meets the eye. Detective Toure searched the internal system. He found articles and video clips extolling the virtue and achievements of the esteemed Deputy Lakos. Under normal circumstances, he would have been extraordinarily impressed. But in the course of a day, the detective was simply disgusted. He felt deceived and defrauded. The man revered and loved by the entire city was someway involved in sheer degradation.

The articles and write-ups spanned a few years. In firsthand interviews, the deputy spoke of how he was able to achieve his success. The reporters wrote about him with what seemed to be authenticity. By all accounts, the people loved him and felt safe with him as the second in command. He was next in line; that was true. The chief was retiring very soon. Steven was the next natural fit and according to his record, he was the most qualified to take the chief's place.

Having already established the public's consensus, Detective Toure was interested in anything that had not hit the public eye.

He pulled up every search engine, including the obscure ones, but all he found were sports-related articles. There were play-by-plays of his time in the pros. His teammates all spoke highly of him. "He was a beast on the court," they said. "He was a true team player. If he was not scoring, he was making plays." Sportscasters and analysts agreed that it was a real tragedy when he was forced to retire. There was no accounting for his injury. Detective Toure looked but found nothing suggesting an injury that occurred before that fateful night's game.

He needed more details. The internal system, as well as the Internet, painted the picture, but Detective Toure knew there was something missing.

He looked around the crowded office area. Crime was obvious obviously up today. The phones rang as dispatchers talked through emergencies. The office bustled from wall to wall. The other detectives were busy, their heads down as they worked on something or simply looked swamped. Scores of people walked in and out of the office with various needs and all sorts of business. All in all, it was a typical day. Detective Toure picked up his phone.

"Senator, it's Detective Toure. Have you grabbed lunch yet?" he asked. "Okay, meet you there."

The detective met Sam at the small dive he and Mina frequented.

"You know, I can't be seen with you much more," the senator began, clearly uncomfortable.

"Don't worry about me. I'm one of your constituents. I'm a voter too," the detective quipped.

Sam started speaking in a hushed whisper. "Don't you think people will start to ask questions?"

"They probably will, but there's nothing to find. Plus, you're good at hiding things. Hide this too," Detective Toure said, putting on his best poker face.

Sam let out a long sigh. "I'm going to make this right," he began. "You can bet your life on that."

"Along those lines, I need your help," the detective spoke a little more warmly.

"With what?" Sam asked.

"I need to see the personnel documentation for the deputy," the detective blurted out.

"Whoa...that's a tall order! All the personnel files are under lock and key with the director of human resources downtown."

"Come on, Senator. I know you know people. You can get us in there for a quick look-see. This is the thing—we need to know who exactly we're dealing with here. Look, I'd prefer if it concludes that Deputy Lakos is a stand-up guy and he recently just fell into some sinful ways. But something tells me that's not what we'll find."

Sam rapped his fingers on the table. "Okay, I get your point—but how does this change anything?" he asked in a hushed yet harsh tone. "Let's say he should be awarded a Nobel Peace Prize. What if he is the next Mother Teresa? Will that change our need to go forward with this operation?"

"You're right. It won't. But the more we know, the better we're prepared. All I need is a quick look. Can't you call for a one-on-one meeting?" Toure rubbed the back of his neck. "Just make something up so they can share this information with you. I'll happen to be waiting in the wings."

"I'm not sure, Detective. If I can do it without drawing attention to myself, okay. But if it looks like it'll be too messy, you'll have to go in blind and hope for the best."

"Fair enough," the detective said. "And what about you? Anything with your assignment?"

"Interesting you should ask, because I was able to halt the confirmation for a little while. I proposed that we wait until one of the members of the Senate is back from an emergency. And then me and the guys will be out of town next week on Thursday and Friday, so that's a further delay. All I could get us was a few more days. The confirmation hearings will continue when we get back, though. Likely on Monday."

"Out of town next week?" the detective asked, quickly intrigued.

"Oh yeah," the senator responded. "It's the Annual Summit on Energy and I am required to go. This is our norm—whoever is going to be out of town, the other two tag along and of course we charge it all to our departments. We're really good at tying it all to public necessity and taxpayer dollars."

"You don't even pay for it out of pocket?" the detective asked.

"No! That's how you play the game. We go and enjoy ourselves and either the state the city or the AG's office pays for it. I forgot—you're not up in that pay grade yet."

Detective Toure furled his brow and scowled. "Just tell me about the trip," he demanded.

"Fine. There's this summit that I invited the guys to months ago. We just confirmed it last week as well."

"Didn't you think it was important to tell us last night?"

The senator shrugged. "No. Why do you care that I have to go to an energy summit?"

The detective threw his hands up and leaned in uncomfortably close to the senator.

"You are going on a scheduled out-of-town visit. You are going with the other two men we are investigating. Don't you think something will happen on that trip?"

Quiet for a moment, Sam shrugged again. "I suppose you are right. So what do you want me to do?"

"It's not really you, Senator. It's us. What will we do?" Detective Toure said and added, "I'll tell you more tonight. By the way, we're meeting at your house later. I hope seven o'clock works." He stood to leave, throwing some crumpled money on the table.

"Oh and those crackers last night were really good," Toure said before departing. "Make sure you have more of them."

***

As promised, Mina, Candace, and Detective Toure met at Senator Kingsly's house that evening. Mina didn't even try to be more pleasant but channeled her aggression and focused her anger. She said a very brief "hello" to the senator when he opened the door. But Candace compensated. Despite protests, she emerged with a large bag of groceries.

"I hope you like pasta," she said.

The senator looked slightly relieved. "I'm glad you showed up with food rather than weapons or authorities."

"Are you still worried about us?" the detective asked.

"I'm worried about her." The senator pointed at Mina.

Detective Toure nodded his head. "You should be. But at least you're finally on the right side. We all have a vested interest in this. But don't take our kindness for weakness. Right, Mina?"

Mina stared at the senator and gave one slow nod of her head.

✠✠

CHAPTER 34: ALLIANCE

Detective Toure tossed and turned for yet another night. Rest did not come easy, if at all. His mind was heavy with a swirl of thoughts. Restless, he felt a pounding in his chest. *This isn't my fight. I didn't sign up for this,* he thought over and over again. He grabbed on to the one thing that he knew would give him solace.

In the darkness and the silence, the detective searched his memories for his grandmother's favorite song. She was a member of the senior choir at United AME Zion Church of Light. She sang all the time. Her high soprano could be heard while she cleaned her house, cooked perfect meals, and attended at family gatherings. Her voice was soothing and Detective Toure reached for the memory that would comfort him in the darkness. He didn't know the words and only remembered the chorus that his grandmother sang over and over. With no concept of the tune and glad that no one else was in the room to witness it, he sang softly, "Precious Lord, take my hand." Those were the only words he remembered, so he sang it over and over again until his heaviness lifted and tiredness overtook him.

Although he was still moons away from a good night's rest, Detective Toure was up and out early for yet another morning. As was his new routine, he stopped for coffee for both he and Deputy Lakos and sat on the precinct bench to wait for him. Stone-faced as usual, the deputy came waltzing in with his shades on. Mustering up all of his energy, Detective Toure offered him a coffee and was ready to work on the missing person's case. The two sat together in the deputy's office. The deputy tried to escort him out a few times but Detective Toure found reasons to stay. He was getting very good at thinking on his feet.

The deputy's cell phone rang. He glanced at it and then looked up to meet the detective's stare. He swiped Ignore on the device and kept on working. His phone rang again.

"Feel free to take that," the detective said. "Don't mind me. I'm busy over here. I'm not really even in the room."

Detective Lakos huffed and picked up his phone. Even his hello sounded cryptic. "Yeah," he whispered. "Tonight. Nine forty-five. Okay."

The detective couldn't help but stare and was relieved that his actions unnoticed. As he worked, he texted the senator. Well aware that cyber conversations never die and are easily monitored, the detective sent a short but sweet text. "9:45?"

Moments later, he received an equally cryptic message.

"Copy."

Detective Toure's mind raced. Was he prepared to go back to that abandoned strip mall and market? He felt as though he'd nearly had a heart attack the last time. He kept his eyes on his files as he pieced things together in his mind. He wanted to have a partner for this endeavor but obviously that would not work. There was no one in the precinct he could trust enough. The two women he trusted could not be seen anywhere near that place. It was too dangerous, although Mina could really hold her own. The telephone interrupted his thoughts. It was an unfamiliar number. Normally he would ignore it, but these days he never knew. Offering no explanation, the detective stood and stepped outside of the office door.

"Hello?" he said quietly.

"Toure, meet me at the HR office. Get there in twenty minutes. I scheduled us a meeting. Follow my lead."

The senator hung up, leaving the detective to search his brain for an excuse. He stepped back into the room and gathered his things.

"Oh, are you going somewhere?" The deputy sounded relieved.

"I was just called in to confer on one of my other cases. I'll be back, though. We're making such great headway." The detective gave him a feeble smile.

"Take your time," the deputy said gruffly. "I'll try not to solve the case without you." He rolled his eyes and went back to work.

Detective Toure checked the time on his cell and rushed to his car. By the time he arrived at the HR office, he had only five minutes to spare. As he walked in, he saw the senator seated and waiting for him.

"Took you long enough!" Sam scolded.

Just then, the HR director entered the waiting area.

"Good afternoon, Senator!" She extended a firm hand to both the senator and to the detective.

"This is my colleague, Detective Toure."

The director nodded his way. "This way, gentlemen."

As they walked behind her, the director began speaking. "You said you needed to see me. You know I'd do anything to ensure your satisfaction, considering how gracious you have been to this department over the years. How can I help you, Senator?"

"Yes, thank you. We have come upon a very sensitive investigation. Unfortunately, one of the officers on the force is being investigated for identity theft. You can see why it was imperative that I see you today."

"Oh no!" she gasped. "Our office does not stand for that. Tell me their name and I will get to the bottom of this immediately!"

The senator shook his head, wringing his hands. "We are already investigating this case. It seems to be tied into a much larger embezzlement issue, which explains why my colleague is here with me. The officer who is now under investigation is allegedly using the identity of our deputy chief— Steven Lakos. Are you familiar with him?"

"In name only. I'm sure I'll get to know him as he will be the chief soon," she responded.

"Oh, I see," the senator continued. "But as I was saying, the identity theft has extended into the deputy's personnel information. We need to check out his file to confirm whether those small details have been copied so that we can thereby prosecute the offending officer."

"Oh my goodness! I completely see the urgency of this matter."

The senator nodded his head in agreement. "If you would be so kind as to allow us to view the file right here in your office we would then be able to continue on with the investigation. Isn't that right, Detective Toure?"

"Exactly that. And we really appreciate your collaboration and assistance in this highly sensitive police matter," the detective said.

"Absolutely! I'll just pull it up on my system and you can view it here for a few moments."

The director tooled around on her computer navigating the information very quickly.

"I'm going to go get a coffee. Would you like one?" the senator asked.

"That would be nice," she smiled.

"Would you like to accompany me?" the senator said offering his arm.

The director looked over at Detective Toure. "Are you okay by yourself, Detective?"

"I'm just fine, thank you for asking. By the time you return with your coffee, I will be finished with my audit."

Sam escorted the director out of her office. Detective Toure quickly jumped into action. Scanning the entire file, he skipped over the mundane details. He went straight to the background check and criminal record. Both were clean. He did find a grievance filed against the deputy and an internal investigation launched with regard to Johannes Maximilian. The report stated that Johannes was improperly processed and the appropriate protocol was not taken, thereby forcing his case to be dismissed. There were another few grievances of similar fashion for other cases. The detective took a picture of the computer screen using his phone. The additional reports outlined both Deputy Lakos's career as a decorated officer and detective and his consistent missteps in criminal prosecution.

"So he would botch the processing knowing that the case would be thrown out. Deep," the detective spoke loudly in his usual fashion.

"What was that, Detective?" the HR director moved steadily back to her desk.

The detective quickly closed the grievance file and reopened the demographics file.

"I'm so sorry. I mumble while I work. I'm all set here. It seemed that the officer in question used only some of his information. He did not assume his entire identity. But that does not place him in any less trouble. Thank you so much for your kindness and accommodations."

The senator also offered many thanks and they exited hastily.

Once outside, the detective extended his hand. "Good work, Senator. Will fill you in tonight."

"Seven o'clock, right?" Sam asked.

"Right."

As he returned to the office, Detective Toure drove on autopilot and let his mind wander. He was entirely wrapped up in the evolution of this case: Oren's death, missing women, rapist on the loose, corruption at the highest of levels. It was nearly too much to process and to work on all at once.

Finally back at his desk, he felt his phone buzz with a text from Mina.

HI, DETECTIVE. YOU'VE BEEN SO COMMITTED TO DOING GREAT WORK AND SHINING IN THE MIDST OF DARKNESS.

I REALLY JUST WANTED TO SAY THANK YOU.

The detective smiled, feeling the depth of each word. He put his phone down on top of a large white envelope. Since he was in his own thoughts he had not even noticed the FedEx envelope waiting on his desk. It was from the state.

He tossed the envelope underneath his arm and walked back out to his car. Once there, he was comfortably protected by the metal that separated him from the outside world. His hands were shaking but there was no one there to see him. He ripped open the envelope and revealed the thirty to nearly forty microfiche reports inside.

Johannes Maximilian had been a very busy man. He was at the helm of a large drug distribution ring on the East Coast. Information in his file connected him to some larger and more serious findings, but it was all circumstantial. As it related to the city, he was implicated in the creation and distribution of an intense new drug. Its street name was SILO. According to the toxicology report, SILO introduces an intense and immediate infection in the brain that causes subservience and intense delusions. It's intended to inhibit the normal fight-or-flight response chemically. Tests have confirmed that prolonged use is identified with early onset of severe mental illness.

According to the case report, SILO was being sold only to establishments. If you did not own a business or run some kind of corporation, it seemed that Johannes would not sell to you. His tactic was more of a warm call, with who you know being very important. He preferred a more high-profile operation and wasn't relegated to street dealings. They were higher-level clientele and therefore the stakes were higher as well. Clients would consume for their own personal pleasures, and also turn over for a profit in their networks. SILO was the newest deadly attraction.

Johannes was a very wealthy man. He was reportedly single now but had been married four times. He had quite a few children with his four wives and it appeared he had a couple of girlfriends. He'd also been prosecuted for a number of charges: federal racketeering, conspiracy, and a laundry list of offenses initiated by the state. He'd served time for racketeering and conspiracy about fifteen years ago. It was considerably less than it could have been. He obviously had a very good attorney. Every charge that was filed in their state since then was dropped due to processing errors.

The detective beat his fist on the steering wheel causing the horn to go off.

"Dammit! How!" he yelled.

He continued reading, getting a sense of the depth of Johannes Maximilian. When he'd exhausted his time away from his desk and had to get back to the office, he folded up his package and shoved it under the seat.

✠✠

CHAPTER 35: DEFEATED

The meeting that night at Sam Kingsly's house was pivotal. Candace again brought food to prepare. Detective Toure appeared worn and tired. He had not yet told Mina and Candace about the impending meeting. 9:45. He did not even want to share this information, but considering he had no one else, he was forced to.

"Mrs. Blake, can I talk to you?" he asked as Sam and Candace prepared food.

"Sure, what's up, Detective?"

"As we get closer to solving the case, I just wanted to check in with you to see if you are all right. Your husband probably knew just about as much as we do now. The mere fact that someone found all of this important enough to kill over makes me nervous for you." He lowered his eyes as he spoke.

Mina reached out her hand and took his. Her hair fell over her shoulders and framed her face well. She looked angelic.

"Detective, I don't know why and I've actually stopped asking. But we were chosen and this is our contribution. Our ancestors pursued truth, justice, and equality. They gave their blood for it. And now it's our turn. Whatever happens, in life or death, it will be okay."

Detective Toure held Mina's hands tightly not wanting to let go. He felt her authority and soothing comfort. Her hands felt electric as they transferred a pulsating and hot new energy through him. His toes started to tingle. The heels of his feet sank deeply into the floor. He felt no separation between his skin, socks, shoes, and the carpet beneath them. The sensation engulfed his legs and proceeded upward to his thighs. His hands and fingers felt electric, too. He wiggled them in Mina's grasp but was careful not to let go. The bulk of his energy settled in his forearms. In concert, the new energy traveled from his shoulders downward to his chest and from his legs transcended to his belly.

Mina's eyes had been closed. "Do you feel that?" she whispered and gave his hands a light squeeze.

The detective didn't speak or move yet exuded a resounding yes. Mina nodded her head in agreement.

Mina let go of his hands when Candace walked in with another culinary spread. The detective pulled back abruptly after catching Candace's watchful eyes. He felt different and stood with an air of confidence he hadn't felt in ages. As he stood, he rolled his shoulders back and held his head a little higher.

Candace brought food to the table and got right to business. Raising her voice, she pounded the table to get everyone's attention. "Listen up! So let me get this straight. We have only a week and a half. After that, Ibra will be confirmed as the new attorney general; Steven Lakos will soon become the chief of police; Oren's murderer will still be at large; and this drug SILO will be accessible and available to cause more women to go missing and to perpetuate rape. Does that sound right? Have I summed it up accurately?" On the brink of tears, Candace's voice quivered as she spoke.

"This can't happen!" she continued. "I'm just as frustrated as you guys are, but you're not doing anything!" She whined again, this time letting a few tears escape.

Surprised by Candace's outburst of emotion, a harsh silence fell over the group. The men looked solemn. Even with his newfound energy, Detective Toure appeared to have had the wind taken out of his sails. He paced back and forth. Sam sat in the corner of the couch looking exasperated as he fanned himself. Mina rocked back and forth, repeating unintelligible words to herself over and over again. The entire group looked like they were moments away from a full-fledged nervous breakdown.

Candace spoke again—more controlled but equally as passionate. "Look at yourselves, guys! This is insurmountable or so it seems. *Come on!* Where's your fight? I don't know about you, but there is no way we can pretend that these few weeks didn't happen. There's no way that I can forget what Ibra tried to do to me. I can't go back to that place of ignorance, I can't."

Mina was the first to respond. She stood up firmly planting her feet beside her and then she lifted her head. She exhaled slowly and began to speak. Her voice was deeper than usual and had an air of coldness.

"They call me Mina. I was once like you, but everything changed the day he left. Now I'm a warrior in a struggle that I can't face alone. Some days I don't know who I am, but I won't stop going until I know the truth. My husband is dead. My best friend, my rock. All because he did his job in the face of chaos. This will end. And although I don't want to, I can do it by myself if I need to. They told me they'll help me. They're here and ready. But it's your turn to live, Senator. And yours too, Detective. Fight and live."

She stopped speaking abruptly and repeated the same words to herself as she played with her necklace.

"Strategy and precision."

Mina walked around the room rotating to each one. She squared up and placed her hands on everyone's shoulders as she spoke.

"This is how it works in command. We pull them in together—Ibra and Steven. We persuade them to implicate each other and we've done all we need to do. From there, they identify the plot against Oren and maybe even the missing. That will eliminate their careers—so no attorney general, no chief of police. And this won't be the way SILO gets out. We already have an in with the senator, and we already have an event. Boys' weekend next week. We will be strategic and play our cards right with a backup plan to the backup plan. We've got this. I won't take *No* for an answer. Or I will do it myself. Take your pick, guys."

Mina paused looking at each directly and intently and closed her eyes.

"We agree," the group said in near unison.

✠

CHAPTER 36: CLARITY

Detective Toure perked up a bit as he digested what Mina said and began to speak slowly. "What you mean is that we're meeting them at boys' weekend, correct, Mrs. Blake?"

"That's exactly what I mean," Mina said.

The time to do just that was fast approaching. None of them seemed inclined to have the detective endure a repeat episode at the abandoned market, so they discussed alternatives.

"Why don't you just go," Candace said to the detective.

"What?" He looked at her as though she'd completely lost her mind. "You should go then, Candace!"

"I would but Ibra would make me out in a heartbeat."

"Wear a disguise then." The detective stared at her without flinching.

"Stop quaking in your boots—man up, and just go!" Candace shouted. "Or, how about you, Senator. You could just record it."

"Are you flipping kidding me?" he said instantly. "Don't you think my buddies would notice me recording them on my phone?"

"Oh, so they're your buddies now! Your criminal rapist murderer buddies!" Candace said.

"We don't know that!" the senator said. "And, there's no way you're getting my voice on any kind of recording with their plan. What about when it comes out that I took the audio of them? Nope. No way. Not gonna happen."

Annoyed, Candace checked the time on her cell phone. She looked stern and was clearly not in the mood for anything from anybody.

"This is the deal," she said. "It's eight-thirty now. Detective Toure, you can go down there now. Hide for a couple of minutes somewhere else and then you can hear everything. That building is huge, and since Sam will be there, he will steer them away from you. Meanwhile, Sam, if you place your phone in your pocket, you can get the entire convo without showing your cards—not even one time." Candace looked triumphant.

"And another thing, Senator," the detective added. "Your buddies are going down. Go ahead and process that. Would you prefer to cooperate with this investigation and basically work against the criminality or be implicated with them when they go down? I can't believe you're considering your reputation now. Now? At this juncture? Funny. Because if Mina didn't stop you, you would have done something truly regrettable." Detective Toure scowled.

9:45.

Sam Kingsly was the first one to walk into the dank building.

"Fellas, why do we always meet in here? It smells like piss."

"We can meet in your apartment next time then. Same smell there too," Steven smirked and walked in behind him.

"Shut up, you two," Ibra said, pushing both of them forward.

Sam reached into his pocket. He felt around for the phone and touched it for security. He was careful not to put his finger over the audio speakers.

Ibra and Steven walked inside and headed to the right this time.

"I wonder what's over here," Steven said as he milled about and walked toward the large open space.

Detective Toure was crouched under a mold-ridden desk twenty-five feet ahead of him. The detective heard footsteps coming his way. The steps came close enough for him to see Steven's image through the cracks in the wood. Toure's heart pounded so hard he thought he might be experiencing the onset of a heart attack. Fear gripped him and his forehead started to sweat profusely. He held his breath, sure that his panting was drawing undue attention. After only a few seconds, his breath was faltering and he knew he had to let it out. Scared that Steven would hear him gasping for air, he looked around frantically to find something to exhale into. The only thing within reach was an old rag. The detective loathed the idea of putting that infested cloth anywhere near his mouth. The steps came closer to the desk as he heard Steven yelling back at the guys.

"I'm coming! What's the freaking rush?"

The detective couldn't last any longer. His eyes watered from the pressure in his chest. He picked up the stiff cloth with two fingers covered by his jacket. He brought it to his lips to blow, just as the Sam walked briskly toward Steven.

"Come on, man! Ibra is waiting on you. We don't have all day for you to play Dora the Explorer," Sam said.

Steven turned to leave and the noise of both of their feet on the linoleum tile echoed as they walked away. The detective dropped the rag and gasped for air in the midst of the ruckus. He leaned back against the legs of the table, not caring about the cobwebs and dirt that got in his hair and on his clothes.

On the other side of the floor, the guys started their meeting. They were far enough away for the detective to remain unseen, but the high ceilings allowed him to hear them clearly and he could still see what was transpiring.

Detective Toure carefully turned off his flash and lifted his phone to capture a picture. He took a few shots; although in the darkness they looked only like clouded blobs.

"Did you try it out?" Ibra asked.

"It works like a charm. Did exactly what you said it would," Sam said.

Steven grabbed Sam's arm. "I don't believe it, man! You tried that? With whom?"

Ibra interjected, stepping in between both of them. "Steven man, why do you have to be in his bedroom?" Ibra stepped back. "But tell us how'd you do it?"

Sam smiled assuredly. "Don't worry about who I did. I'm telling you, slipped it into a mixed drink and it was absolutely no problem. Plus, the chick thought her condition was due to her one drink. Have these girls second-guessing themselves with this."

Ibra nudged him on the back and looked at Steven. "See? I told you! I knew this would be easy. Look here, we can take this and anyone with the right price and the right credentials can get it directly from us. You have no idea how much money and power this ticket will bring!"

Steven shrugged his shoulders and nodded his head in approval. "We're taking this on the road next week?"

"Absolutely. There are some women who will never see this coming. You can have anything you want from them or take what you want and leave the rest," Ibra said.

"I want in on this guys," Sam said. "I'm not exactly sure what you guys do, but I want in. Boys' weekend after my conference. I get first dibs."

Ibra put his arm around Sam and Steve's shoulders. "No problem, man. You're in. No questions asked, though, not until we give you the go ahead."

"Okay. I can do that."

"I'll see you guys in a few days then." Ibra high-fived them and slipped out the front door to his waiting vehicle.

Steven turned to Sam. "This is not for the faint of heart. You might want to put on your big-boy drawers before you get there."

"I'll be ready for you, Steven," Sam said. "Don't you worry about me."

The next few days moved quickly. The detective barely had time to catch his breath. He was working the missing person's case, an additional existing caseload, and keeping very close tabs on Deputy Steven Lakos. He was exhausted but felt accomplished. He knew what he had to do and he was working hard to prepare for it.

***

Mina found peace at the altar she'd built in her bedroom. She started small with a table and white tablecloth. The more she communed with her own energy, the more she felt led to add additional pieces to the altar. She added the ornate wooden box that the thumb drive had previously been in. She added spices, cleansing water, candles, and pictures. Occasionally, she brought a favorite food to the altar as well. Her most important work was the time she spent daily communing with herself through Eshu and Yemaya.

Over the course of a few days, Mina noticed an even more extensive transformation. Her nose widened ever so slightly, and her lips became fuller. Her face was more slender and her overall muscle tone increased. It was during a regular examination of her features that she identified a faint scar over her eyebrow. She rubbed it with her fingertips, feeling the indentation of the skin. She knew that she had not fallen or tripped or otherwise scraped herself. Yet as she stood rubbing that physical reminder, she saw it clearly. She saw herself running alongside a throng of men and women. Her sword was drawn, but it did not protect her faithfully. An additional sword cut through the air aiming directly at her face. She sidestepped and avoided the brunt of the blow, but it caught her eyebrow. Her opponent drew the sword back with the intention of thrusting again. But instead, Mina blocked the oncoming sword with her own and in double time, thrust her sword into the opponent's chest. She felt the life of another dissipate immediately. Now, looking steadily in the mirror, she rubbed her wound. It felt fresh as if the skin was currently broken.

Mina prepared herself for battle.

✠✠

CHAPTER 37: EXECUTION

Mina entered the gym with her bag in tow. She saw Kimber on the mat doing floor exercises in the adjoining room. Mina waved to the man covering the reception area and walked along without waiting for an invitation.

"Glad to see you!" Kimber said scrambling to her feet. She trotted over to where Mina stood in the middle of the floor. Mina grinned and outstretched her arms to embrace her.

"Guess who I found," Kimber called over to her trainer. She pointed her finger at Mina and poked her a little bit in the process.

"Ouch! Really Kimber? Is that how you treat your guests?" Mina laughed and poked her back.

"No, but you're no guest now, are you? In any case, he's been asking about you since you came in here last time." She pointed her finger in the direction of the trainer.

"I figured that you've been busy but it's really cool to see you," Kimber continued. "Wow, look at you? You look different, lady. Can't put my finger on it. Still a knockout, though. Speaking of which—you ready to do some working out?"

"Sure am. That's why I brought this bag me." Mina tapped her bag.

The next hour and a half were spent on strength training and techniques with the trainer. At the end of the session, the trainer said, "Why don't we do some of our ancient art?"

Mina clasped her hands and bowed. "Absolutely," she responded and moved into position.

True to form, Mina slid through the air with kicks and low floor swipes. She danced with the trainer as he exhibited similar form. All the while, Mina interacted as the drums were beating. She heard the rhythmic steady beat and moved in concert with it. The trainer must have tapped right in as well. Although in seeming opposition, they moved together. Mina's arms filled the entire room with her movement. Her gracefulness was not easily matched. At the end of the session, she bowed and hugged the trainer.

"Every time I watch you, I learn more. Every time we spar, it feels more like a dance." Mina grinned.

As she spoke, her energy was high. There was even a distinct glow around her. The trainer felt the air above her head as he moved his hands through the air just outside of her neck, shoulders, and arms.

"Your aura is magnificent," he marveled. "But that's the way it should be," he continued. "If I don't bring you deeper and higher, then you have not been able to engage in the art. Tell me again how this came to you."

"I wish I could," Mina said. "I just felt it. And once I felt it, my body was obedient."

"That is so cool, man," Kimber said. "I've trained for years and on occasion, I don't have to think about my next move. Sometimes, I know exactly what my opponent is going to do and I think ahead to counter that. But I have never felt able to execute based on my body coming into agreement with my spirit. Wow. With that kind of alignment, I would never lose a match."

"That's where the real power lies. We really do have some things to talk about." Mina beamed.

Kimber shook her head in agreement and clapped her hands slowly. "Miss Mina, are you back with me tomorrow? I'm doing legs. Good opportunity to tighten those already tight hammies."

"I wouldn't miss that for anything, Miss Kim. So, until then?" Mina gathered her things to leave the room. She stopped midway and turned around. Kimber and the trainer were still watching her. She bowed a second time and mouthed the words "Thank you," before she headed home.

***

Electrified, Mina bounded into her house, flinging the door open.

"Candy! Candy!"

"I'm right here, Mina."

Candace was seated on the couch. Her legs were sprawled out and she was draped over the edge almost touching the floor. Her head hung backward and she stared at the ceiling.

"Candace, are you okay? What's going on here? Did something happen?" Mina demanded.

Candace appeared exasperated. She sat up and faced Mina. Her face was streaked with tears; her mascara had run and her eye shadow was blotchy. She did not look like her normal, radiant self.

"Candy! Oh my God! Are you hurt?" Mina cried.

Candace started to whimper. "No, I'm not hurt. I just got off the phone with my auntie. She was checking on you actually. But then we got to talking and…"

Candace dropped her face in her hands.

"And what?" Mina asked.

Candace didn't lift her head but instead recounted the story through clasped hands.

"She told me more about my family. Remember I was so curious. So here it is: They suspected there was divination involved and that incantations were spoken over me when I was a child." She lifted her head finally. "Auntie told me there was a priest who tried to bless me as a Christian but could not go forward with it." The tears streamed down her face. "According to Auntie, he felt something so powerful about me that he did not want to be involved. That was when Baba took me to the Ifa priest. The Ifa priest told my Baba that I would embrace my legacy and my life would be in line with my name. He basically spoke a prophecy over me." She sniffed. "I'm told that my destiny is one of triumph and challenge, all to bring people together. My auntie said this was supposed to manifest in my life sometime after the age of thirty. That was when I was renamed Candace." She paused and took a breath. Mina grasped her hand. "And as an aside," she continued, "have you ever heard of Queen Candace? According to my family, I share the same spirit guide as her. Auntie said I'll know when this transformation occurs. I will feel a strength and a conviction that are not my own. When that happens I should be prepared to take up training and instruction. That's crazy, Mina. Absolute foolishness, right?"

Mina sat down, still holding her friend's hand. She saw the fear in Candace's eyes. It was a fear that she knew too well. Mina was able to empathize knowing that she was now in the process of embracing herself and had just freed herself from that same fear.

"You know, Candy, you don't have to do anything you don't want to. Even if Auntie suggested that this is your destiny and that the essence of the Queen will inhabit you, you can choose whether or not to accept it. There's always a choice. Always," Mina said rubbing the palms of Candace's hands.

"How can I say *no* to my destiny?" she wailed. "Isn't that like a challenge to the space-time continuum or some craziness like that? Won't that ensure that there is a crack in our existence?"

"What? Where did you even hear that from?" Mina laughed. "Then again, never mind. But back to the point—it's your choice, Candy. You can be whoever you want to be. The spirit, the essence is just there to encourage and guide you. If you choose to embrace your royal ancestry and perhaps the guidance of our ancestors, then your life will be different. If you choose to ignore it all then that's all right too."

"But, Mina, I'm scared. What if this changes me? Remember who I am…well, I guess who I thought I was? I have no room in my life for the religion of our ancestors."

Mina reached out to Candace and stroked her hair. "You don't have to make any decisions today," she spoke calmly. "And you don't need to explain yourself to me. You're my best friend and I got your back. The same way you have had my back this whole time."

"And why did my aunt just tell me now? I should have had two years to prepare for this."

"Really, Candy?" Mina frowned. "You know you. If Auntie told you at any point before today, you would have obsessed about it for years. I really think it's for the best. But I have one thing to suggest: *feel* it—don't *think* about it. Oh, by the way," Mina added, "did Auntie have anything to say about me?"

"It's not always about you, Mina!"

"Sheesh. Sorry I asked." Mina hit Candace playfully.

They stayed up talking that night and explored their convictions, religious beliefs, fears, and drives.

"I think once you experience the wholeness of our Orisha you will be at peace."

Candace nodded. Mina's cell phone buzzed interrupting their conversation.

"Good evening, Detective," Mina said. "Is everything all right tonight? Let me put you on speaker."

"Hi, ladies," Detective Toure began. "As I was saying, I have some more information on Johannes Maximilian. Looks like he had a case that our friend the deputy handled a few years back. The department confiscated some of his drugs and drug paraphernalia. It was called SILO even back then, and Johannes was more regularly known as Max. So this SILO was in production and Max had just begun distributing to high-end clients. The detective handling the case was Steven Lakos. Surprise, surprise!"

"Unbelievable!" said Candace.

Detective Toure continued. "He arrested Max, processed him, and confiscated the items. The reports also state that the confiscated drugs went missing and Max was also able to walk right out the front door of the precinct."

Mina shook her head as she listened.

"The interesting part about all of this is there was a rival drug lord who made and distributed a drug similar to SILO. I don't remember his name. But he distributed to anyone – high end, low end, didn't matter. And it was way cheaper, too. He was making a mint of his production.

"What? How were they making this? Mina asked. "So not just one synthesized SILO drug on the streets, but two? I don't get it."

"Insane, right? But get this," the detective continued, "Once Max walked out, this new guy, his competition, turned up dead just a day later. He was found with his car in a ditch. They said he had run off the road into a ravine. He was pronounced dead at the scene. They concluded it was the driver's error. But I saw two inconsistent reports that noted tampering with the engine and brakes."

"Are you serious?" Mina said barely above a whisper.

"I'm afraid I am. Seems that car tampering and Max are coincidentally linked."

"I don't believe in coincidences," Mina replied.

"Am I hearing this right?" asked Candace. "The drug kingpin Max might be linked to Oren's murder?"

"And who exactly do they have in common?" the detective prompted.

"Deputy Steven Lakos," Candace said.

"On another note," Detective Toure continued, "I talked to the senator earlier. His reservations are made. He gave me his hotel name and his flight itinerary. Ibra and Steven will be staying in the same hotel in adjoining rooms and will be on the same flight.

Can you ladies make a reservation for the night before? I think it best that we all travel together."

"Sounds good to me," Candace said.

"I'll take care of that tonight. We are definitely ending this," Mina spoke with a tremble that Candace had not heard in weeks.

Once the detective hung up, Mina retreated to her room. She gave thanks at the altar and then began a cleansing ritual. Less stressed than when she walked into the room, Mina lay on her bed. She curled up in a ball and cried.

"Oren, my heart aches for you. This hole feels like it will never be filled. It grows and the missing pieces never replaced."

As she lay crying, she felt a weight on her exposed side. With eyes still closed, Mina identified the warmth and the weight of the presence. The presence wrapped around her in a peaceful manner. The distinct smell was a mix of sandalwood and mint; Dolce & Gabbana cologne filled her nostrils. Mina wept until she fell asleep.

✠✠

CHAPTER 38: BOYS' WEEKEND

Mina and Candace waited impatiently. Mina paced near the front door checking the window every five minutes. Candace made a lot of noise in the kitchen. She baked muffins, bagged them, separated the flavors, and wrote their names on each one's own personal stash. After baking, she went about cleaning the kitchen from top to bottom.

"Candy, how are you making that much noise! I can't hear myself think. I won't be able to hear the detective when he blows the horn."

"He's not due to be here for a half hour, Mina."

"What if he is running late? How will we get to the airport? Let me run real quick and put gas in my car." Mina grabbed her purse.

Candace stormed out of the kitchen and placed her hands on Mina's shoulders. "I see it's my turn to be the voice of reason. Although I've made every variety of muffins I could, I'm not nervous. I suppose I have conflicting energy, but I'm ready. I'm ready as if my life depends on it. You're ready too, Mina. Just take a deep breath."

"Can I make you a cocktail? How about a vodka and cranberry?" Candace asked.

Before Mina had the opportunity to kindly reject the offer, Candace was back in the kitchen clamoring away. She returned in moments with a beautifully made drink. "I made one for myself as well," she said, "but I already drank it."

Mina sank into her couch, closed her eyes, and began to breathe deeply. She took small sips of her drink but primarily concentrated on her breathing. Candace retreated into the kitchen to occupy herself some more.

The doorbell rang, startling Mina. Candace rushed to the front door before Mina was even able to stand.

"Detective! We've been waiting. Would you like some muffins?" Candace pushed the bag of muffins toward him. On it, his name was carefully inscribed.

The detective offered his thanks and picked up a duffel bag that was by the door. Mina was right behind him once he turned to leave.

"Come on, Candy. And so it begins!" she called.

Their departing flight was without issue. Detective Toure, Mina, and Candace sat in the same row. The detective was at one end and Mina was at the other. Candace was more than happy to be in the middle. That allowed her to be in constant communication with whoever was paying her the most attention. She chatted with the detective for most of the flight.

It was Wednesday night. The senator was not due in until Thursday afternoon according to his itinerary. Detective Toure had shied away from calling him. Sam was being accommodating and cooperative so the detective started to take it a little easy on him. Nevertheless, he monitored him in a variety of ways, none of which he actually shared with the senator.

The delegation for the energy summit was massive. Elected officials and representatives from state agencies from everywhere in the United States came together to engage in a two-day conference. The venue was ripe for Attorney Ibra Marcus and Deputy Steven Lagos to strike.

The hotel and conference center was hopping with guests. Even for a Wednesday night there were lines for every service you could imagine. Obtaining late-night snacks was more of a chore than a treat.

Against Mina's better judgment, they decided to all share a room. The detective convinced her that for the benefit of health and safety it would be for the best. Mina had not shared a bed with anyone other than Oren in a great number of years. The last time she'd done so was when she was a child and went on trips to see Grandmother. During these visits, her cousins were also in attendance and ultimately, a few of them shared a bed. But Mina was grown now. She had no desire to share a bed with anyone, even her best friend. For the sake of peace and ease, though, she consented.

Once in the room, the detective announced that he was calling it a night. He looked exhausted. And why wouldn't he? The last few weeks had not allowed a lot of time for sleep. He slipped into the bathroom and put on a two-piece pajama outfit.

Mina thought he looked cute. He reminded her of the way she expected middle-aged men on TV to dress for bed. He climbed right into his bed, closest to the window, and rolled over.

Candace and Mina still had loads more adrenaline that wouldn't allow them to go to sleep for the moment.

Candace looked at her phone. "Mina it's only nine o'clock. Let's go downstairs to the lounge."

Mina generally would not have agreed, but there was no way she was going to bed.

"Let's go," she said grabbing her purse.

They checked out their surroundings. It was kind of drab at first glance. The interior looked old and there was a hint of decay in the air. Music was piped through the lounge's sound system. It was not lively at all. The only thing going for the spot was that the bartender was very capable and entertaining. Candace walked up to the bar.

"Can we have two vodkas and cranberry, please?" she asked with a wink.

The bartender smiled and started talking to them about where they were from.

Candace and Mina had not considered using aliases or changing their backstory. Instead, they agreed to use their real names during the trip and even shared their actual hometown with the bartender. Oblivious to anything unique about them, the bartender continued to make their drinks.

"Can I change the music?" Candace asked politely.

"Knock yourself out, love. Anything for Miss Candace," the bartender replied.

Candace climbed over the bar and landed beside the bartender. She fiddled around until she found some lively music. It woke the bar up. The previously despondent crowd was up and moving on the makeshift dance floor. Candace and Mina ordered one more round of drinks. By this time, the bar was really filling up. The music blasted and the people welcomed the party. The bartender took out the microphone.

"Glad you're having a good time tonight! When you see this lovely lady give her a big thanks for the music—Miss Candace!"

Men and women all over the bar raised their glasses and bottles in Candace's direction. Obviously pleased with herself, Candace raised her own glass as well.

"Ready babes?" Mina asked.

"Sure am," Candace responded, taking a swig of her drink.

They left the bar and returned to their room. The detective snored lightly. His exhaling resembled the rustling of a small animal. He was more cute than annoying. Candace went to the bathroom to change for bed. She returned wearing a very short and tight pink teddy. Mina had taken the liberty of changing right there facing the detective's back. She wore yoga pants and a sweatshirt.

"What?" Mina whined. "Don't you have anything else?"

"No," Candace answered defensively. "You know this is how I sleep."

"But what about the detective? Don't get yourself in trouble here, Candy," Mina warned her.

"Don't worry about him. I'm an early riser. I'll be up and dressed before he even opens his eyes."

Mina smirked.

The next morning Mina rolled over and bumped into Candace. She jumped up quickly forgetting they had shared a bed. She sat up and watched her best friend sleep peacefully although snoring like a freight train. She stretched and rolled her neck, rotated her ankles, and bent her knees to get the blood flowing.

"Good morning, Mrs. Blake." Detective Toure sat on the rolling chair at the hotel's writing desk. He was fully dressed down to his suit jacket and dress shoes.

"Good morning, Detective. Did you rest well? I hope we weren't too loud for you."

"No, I was just fine. This was the best rest I've had in a long time."

Candace sat up looking slightly disheveled. Her teddy although on, was not covering much. Her bare chest was clearly visible. The detective looked at her but quickly spun his chair away toward the window.

"Candy, your clothes!" Mina called out.

Candace quickly adjusted herself and popped out of bed to the bathroom. She ran the water and emerged about twenty minutes later fully dressed and made up. She was ready to go. Both the detective and Candace looked at Mina expectantly.

"Well, aren't you going to get ready?" Candace asked.

Mina shot her the famous disapproving look and got up.

The detective faced the window again. He called over his shoulder.

"The senator just texted. They're here."

✠✠
CHAPTER 39: CONFERENCE

Sam was scheduled to attend the conference all day. It was a high-profile affair and the who's who of politics would definitely be watching. Ibra and Steven, on the other hand, were simply along for the ride.

"You know where we'll be, Sam. When you wrap up for the day come grab us for dinner," Ibra said.

"Yeah I know. Poolside or barside. You guys are nothing if not consistent."

"Have fun. We know you political types get all worked up over dumb stuff. This time, you're Captain Planet, huh?" Steven said.

Ibra and Steven burst out in laughter as they approached their rooms.

"Laugh it up, but you'll be glad when you can fill your gas guzzler with synthetic fuels rather than depleting the natural resources of our planet."

"Oh my God! Give it a rest, dude," Steven yelled from inside his room.

"Whatever, guys. On that note, I'm gone." Sam dropped his things off in his room and exited even more quickly.

Ibra walked over to Steven's room. "Why don't you let up on him a bit, man?"

"Steven leaned up against his wall with his hands behind his neck. Good question, brother. I just don't like him. I know he's been your friend forever and is mine by default. But something about him has always rubbed me the wrong way. Always has."

"Don't worry about Sam. He's wanted to be a part of anything we're doing for a seriously long time. I think he's just happy to be here."

"Shouldn't it be the other way around? Shouldn't we be the ones happy to tag along?" Steven asked.

"No, not this time. Cause we could have proceeded with anybody with this new street rollout, but we chose him. He should feel honored. But in any case, try to go a little easier on him."

"Fine, man. I got you. The same way I always have."

Ibra patted Steven on the back and went back to his room.

A few hours later, Candace and Mina were still in their hotel room. Mina relaxed under the blankets. Candace flipped channels while lying on the bed.

"Nothing on. Just goofy daytime TV. How do people watch this?" Candace scowled and threw the remote on the bed.

"Mina, I'm bored. I can't sit here and wait for the night to come. Can't we take a walk or something? C'mon. Let's stretch our legs."

Mina flipped back the covers in one fell swoop.

"Whatever we're doing has to happen now. If not, I'm taking a nap. Want to go work out, Candy? I'm missing a training day today anyway." Mina admired her own body, running her hands over her well-defined abs and muscular thighs.

"Uh, no thanks. You've revved up your training and you're officially out of my league now."

"Why don't you two go by the pool?" Detective Toure lifted his head from behind his laptop. "Just don't draw attention to yourselves."

"The pool?" Mina said. "I thought you wanted us all to lay low."

"I do. But truthfully, Mrs. Blake, no one will recognize you. You look vastly different than you did even a few months ago. And you're miles away from home. Candace, on the other hand, wear a hat or something." The detective looked Candace up and down. She wore a very tight pants outfit leaving little to the imagination.

Mina threw Candace a beach hat. "Put this on."

"What? Are you serious?" Candace frowned.

They gathered their pool gear and left.

"Candy, the detective still doesn't know about you and Ibra. Let's keep it that way, please."

"You think we'll run into them?"

"Doubt it, but if you see him, pinch me. I've only seen his pictures. Steven doesn't know either of us, though, so that should be fine."

They found a secluded spot at the rear of the pool area. Candace scooted ahead and secured a table and umbrella combo. There were a few other folks, primarily couples, reclining on the pool chairs. Mina grabbed a complimentary newspaper and wandered to the edge of the pool. She sat on the edge dangling her legs in the water. She was the only one in the water so she was able to splash and kick.

"Mina, aren't you worried about your hair getting wet? Oh yeah. Forget I asked," Candace said as she played on her phone.

Mina was engrossed in the book review section of the paper when a huge gush of water splashed her. It wet her entirely and drenched the newspaper she was reading. She looked away annoyed and felt around for the towel beside her. As she dried her face, a sultry, deep voice interrupted her.

"Oh my God! Ma'am, we are so sorry."

Mina looked up into the gorgeous face of Ibra Marcus. He stood in the water at her feet. He intently gathered the limp pages that had fallen into the water and folded the remaining paper into quarters. "My buddy over there dared me to cannonball and neither of us saw you. Although it's amazing that neither of us did considering how radiant you are."

He flashed her a smile to die for and sat there staring at her. Before Mina was able to open her mouth she felt a solid tap to the back of the head.

"Ouch!" Mina said

The culprit, a balled up towel, was also beside her.

"Sorry," a muffled, distorted voice uttered behind her.

Mina turned to see Candace trying her best to cover her face with the broad brim hat. She fiddled uncomfortably. All that was exposed were her wide-open, unmistakably fear-filled eyes.

Mina quickly turned around glad to find Ibra still busy with folding the newspaper.

"That's kind of you to say," Mina said anxiously. Her heart started to beat quickly. "That's all right, though. This is a pool so that should be expected."

Mina rolled to her knees to stand.

"Hold on there. Gone so soon?" Ibra asked.

"Yeah. I was wrapping up anyway."

"Can I buy you dinner later? Let me buy you dinner. That's the least I could do."

Mina smiled sweetly. "I'm sorry. I have dinner plans." She moved in the direction of the exit.

Ibra hoisted himself out of the pool quite athletically and trotted to her side. He immediately blocked her path. "Okay. A drink then?"

Mina paused reflectively. "I could do that."

"Perfect. Meet me at the bar right on the mezzanine."

"Sounds great. What time?" she asked.

"Nine forty-five."

Mina nodded and Ibra stepped aside allowing her to pass. Once outside of the pool area, she saw Candace's back a few paces in front of her. Candace moved quickly to the elevators with a towel wrapped around her body and head held low. She held the beach hat firmly on her head.

Mina slammed their room door accidentally as she leaned on it.

"I can't believe it!" she screamed as Candace crawled to the bed. "Of all the people in this hotel…" she continued.

Candace was visibly shaken and hadn't spoken a word.

Mina rambled on and recounted the entire ordeal to the detective. "I can see why people are so drawn to him. He's magnetic and charismatic."

"Not you now," Candace said weakly.

"No! I'm not falling for that psychopath!" Mina countered.

"You've got to be really weak-minded to fall for Ibra Marcus," the detective said. "Regardless of how good he might look or how successful he is." He continued to work on his laptop.

Candace rolled over on the bed and moaned.

"Well the bottom line is that he has secured the perfect setup for us to make our move tonight," Mina said defiantly.

✚✚
CHAPTER 40: MEETING

It was 9:30 p.m. Mina was dressed to the nines. Her makeup was more than she was used to, but Candace convinced her that it was a necessity. Her hair was flawless. She was the whole package.

Earlier in the evening, she had taken quiet time outside of the room to invoke her spirit. Mina wandered the grounds desperate for fresh air. She closed her eyes and felt the air on her neck. It whipped around her body as the temperature dropped. Clouds amassed and the sky darkened before it opened up allowing a few drops of rain to fall, which thrilled Mina to no end. Standing outside the hotel, she stuck out her tongue to catch a few. She wanted to twirl and run but recalled the detective's admonition to draw no attention to herself.

Instead, she breathed in the smell of rain and reveled as it connected with her face. Embracing her own duality as Aminatu, she acknowledged her ancestors, the Orisha energy, particularly Eshu and Yemaya, and her own being. Quieting her thoughts, she envisioned the end. She saw blood run to the point that she tasted it in her mouth. She licked her lips convinced that she still tasted it. She saw her desire and felt it deeply inside. Mina reached her hands up to feel the elements and immediately experienced a charge that reverberated up and down her spine. She shivered as she experienced distinct coolness on the back of her neck.

She narrowed her vision and her hazel eyes darkened to black. "*Now*, I'm ready," she whispered confidently.

Mina walked to the mezzanine floor and into the bar by herself. She found a seat at the bar and flagged the waitress down to order seltzer water. The room was dimly lit and soft jazz played in the background. It looked dead again with just a few people in the room—but it was early, Mina thought.

In a far dark corner, Mina saw the familiar backs of both Detective Toure and Candace. They had their backs to the open area of the bar and were nestled in each other's arms. The detective was wearing a baseball cap and black turtle neck. Candace wore an understated black sweater and had her hair uncharacteristically pinned up. She leaned on the detective's shoulders, able to see behind him through the crevices in their bodies.

Right on cue at 9:45 p.m., the three men walked into the bar. Sam looked uneasy when he saw Mina and completely averted eye contact.

Steven and Sam took a seat in a booth. Ibra walked right over to Mina and slid into the stool beside her.

"It'd be impossible not to notice you. You are a gem," Ibra whispered in Mina's ear.

"Why thank you," Mina said beaming. "How are you tonight?"

"Not too bad. Much better now." He smiled and grabbed lightly at Mina's hand.

"Bartender, can we have a few drinks?" Ibra fiddled in his jacket pocket as he spoke.

The bartender came over and stood by them.

"Hey, I remember you from last night," he said.

"Oh yeah," Mina replied nervously willing him to go away.

"Where's your friend? The funny one. What's her name again?"

Mina cocked her head to the side and looked at him like she had no idea who or what he was talking about.

Sam walked up to the bar and stood alongside Ibra, interrupting the conversation.

"Hey!" He placed a firm hand on Ibra's shoulder.

"Can I buy your friend a drink?" he asked very suggestively.

Ibra donned a puzzled expression that faded into knowing.

"Ohh…yeah. Sure," he said slowly.

Sam waved to the bartender. "Buddy, can I have a shot of whiskey and a tequila on the rocks for my friend and for the lady?" Sam's eyes connected with Mina's with great assurance.

"I'd like a vodka and cranberry please," Mina requested.

"There you have it. Thanks." He nodded to the bartender.

The bartender returned quickly with the drinks in hand. As he laid them down, Ibra slipped something under Sam's hands. He tried to be inconspicuous, but Mina watched his every move. Sam nodded vigorously as he spoke, although it was quite unnecessary.

"Ahh, that's perfect timing. I'm sure we can all use a drink," Sam said reaching for his.

Ibra got out of his stool and stood uncomfortably close to Mina. He leaned over the bar blocking Sam from her view.

Sam pulled Mina's drink close to him.

"Tell me about yourself," Ibra began. "How is it that a diamond such as yourself got stuck at a boring political event?

"I'm a financial consultant. It pays for us to know things like how the financial environment will be affected by the shift in our energy policies." The words rolled off Mina's tongue succinctly, thoroughly impressing her company.

"Wow. Financial genius. Money guru. My kind of woman," Ibra stammered. "Sam, pass the drink to the lady."

Sam passed it down and Mina took a few sips before pushing the glass away.

"What's the matter? Why aren't you drinking it?" Ibra said, pushing the glass closer to Mina.

Sam was deeply engaged in a conversation with a chatty man beside him and paid no attention to Mina or Ibra.

"I will. Taking my time, though," Mina responded.

"We might not have time. Have some more. Loosen you up," Ibra said.

Mina obliged and drank the majority of her drink.

"That's a good girl," he said.

"What's up with this music?" Annoyed, Ibra flagged down the bartender.

The bartender shrugged his shoulders and kept at the drink he was making.

Ibra leaned in closer to Mina. "Tell me about you. I'm so intrigued by you already. I want to hear everything. Let's start with your name."

"Wow, I guess we hadn't done that part yet. My name is Mina."

The bartender picked up his head. "Now I remember. Your name is Mina and your friend is Candace. You guys are from the city right?"

"What?" Ibra questioned.

Mina started to get warm.

"Candace? Is she in here?" Ibra demanded.

Oblivious, the bartender kept talking. "Yeah, she's in the corner over there." The bartender pointed to where Candace and the detective were sitting.

The bartender took out the cordless mic from underneath the bar.

"Candace! Candace! Come on over here and turn this into a dance party again! Everybody, give Miss Candace a hand!"

Instinctively Candace turned her head at the sound of her name. People all over the bar clapped and cheered at the bartender's insistence.

"What the—*That's* your friend?" Ibra yelled to Mina.

Candace turned away quickly from Ibra's stare and grabbed her things to go.

"What the hell is going on here? You know who I am, don't you, Mina?" he said, huffing.

Mina gathered her confidence and looked him right in the eye. "Yes, I do."

"What's your real name? Who are you?" he spoke harshly and gritted his teeth.

He grabbed her wrist tightly from under the bar. "And you better tell me the truth before I snap your wrist right here."

Mina winced in pain.

"What's your name?" he asked again slowly and deliberately.

Leaning in to Mina, he placed a hard object near her ribcage.

Mina breathed out deeply. Poised and controlled, she looked directly into Ibra's eyes. "My name is Aminatu Cisse Blake, but they call me Mina."

Ibra smiled wildly. "Aminatu Blake. Wow. BLAKE. Get up and walk to the door."

He forced the narrow object deeper into her ribcage.

"Don't run. Don't do anything stupid or we'll both be sorry."

Mina stood and walked with Ibra's arm around her. He ushered her out the door quickly. They walked through the front door and down the ramp to the parking lot. Steven ran up behind them.

"Get the van. Now!" Ibra yelled at him. "Meet me at the side. Unloading."

Steven ran off to the covered parking deck.

"Aminatu Blake, huh. Okay, that's what's happening? All right. We'll take care of this right now," Ibra rambled on like a madman, pacing and talking to himself, all the while dragging Mina with him, hanging on to her arm so tightly she cried out.

"My arm!"

"Shut up!" he said in hushed tones.

"Ibra!" Candace screamed. "What are you doing?" Candace bolted from around the corner to where they stood outside.

She ran full speed ahead. As she neared where they stood, Ibra pulled back and extended a balled fist. It connected right with Candace's jaw. The momentum and the blow knocked her five feet to the left and squarely on her back.

"Candy!" Mina wriggled herself free and ran to her side.

By this time, Sam had left the bar as well and joined them outside. Seeing Candace on the ground writhing in pain, he ran to her.

✠✠

CHAPTER 41: AMINATU

"Oh my God! Ibra did you just hit her? Is she unconscious?" Sam said stunned.

"Oh…no. Never that," Ibra said, laughing. "Actually, she simply bumped into me when she was running. See? She's moving." He laughed harder as he looked at Candace rolling on the ground.

A van pulled up with Steven in the driver's seat.

Ibra grabbed at Mina's arm and yanked her up. He looked at Candace rolling on the ground holding her face.

"Don't worry about Mrs. Oren Blake. I won't hurt her. We're gonna have a good time. Trust me." Ibra bowed to Candace and Sam.

Ibra yanked at Mina and pushed her through the side door of the van. Steven started to drive off before the doors were even closed properly.

Once they rounded the corner, Detective Toure emerged instantly from the parking lot driving a small gray coupe.

"Get in!" the detective yelled.

Sam lifted Candace and placed her in the back seat.

"Did you see that?" Sam yelled.

"I saw the whole damn thing," the detective said shaking his head.

He enabled an app on his phone and a GPS tracker was activated. "Thank God she still has her phone," Detective Toure said.

"But did you get it?" Candace moaned from the back seat.

"I sure did," Sam said holding up the packet of white pills and pill dust that Ibra had slipped to him at the bar.

***

Mina sat uncomfortably on the floor of the van.

A thick cord wrapped around her wrists and ankles secured her in place. It was tied individually and the remnants of cord were tied together. The cord was wrapped a few times around itself but done loosely. Ibra was still rambling on incoherently. He appeared to be in a heightened state— his own endorphins, which probably accounted for the sloppy tying job. Mina didn't wiggle or make a sound. She remained where her captors had placed her.

"What's up with you, Blake?" Ibra held Mina's face. His hand was soft but his grip on her chin was hard. He caressed her cheeks. He licked his finger and slid it across Mina's lips then slapped her with an open hand.

"You gonna play nice for Daddy, baby?"

Feeling the sting on her cheek and heat of his breath, Mina forced her eyes closed.

He threw her shoulders down, forcing her to slam her head as she fell to the floor. She lay in front of him, motionless, her eyes closed. Her head started to throb and she regretted the few moments when she opened her eyes.

Ibra turned his attention to Steven. "Is the spot all set up?"

"Not fully, but we don't need much."

Mina heard a flip and click close to her ear. She felt a cold instrument glide along her neck. Ibra was careful not to puncture her skin. Instead, he produced a long steel blade and sliced the thin straps of her dress. The material fell to the floor on either side. He gripped her dress and yanked it down exposing her bra. With one more slice to the bra straps, he revealed her naked breasts.

"Steven, I'm helping you out! You won't need to do this part tonight. You can get right to the action."

"I know you want first crack at this one. You have more connection to her than I do...considering her husband and all. By the way, ma'am, my name is Steven Lakos and I will be taking full advantage of you tonight."

They both cackled in a maniacal manner and high-fived each other. The skin on Mina's scalp grew cold and she cringed listening to them laugh.

"She's quiet, though. It must be taking effect. Jo-Max has outdone himself with this new formula," Ibra said.

"I'll let him know that you approve," Steven replied.

Mina remembered that she was supposed to be significantly drugged. Although not affected by their drugs, Ibra's touch placed her in a unique stupor.

She moaned genuinely and her breathing became even more shallow. She held her breath for a few moments. Seconds later she coughed violently to recoup the needed oxygen. She opened her eyes slightly and saw Ibra leaning over her. His eyes shone in the darkness. His pupils were dilated and nearly black. Mina intended on engaging in sport with Ibra, as she and her team discussed last night. In their strategy, Mina planned on casually retaliating in the moment, but Ibra's heartlessness brought her to terror. His coldness was effortlessly transferred to her space and his energy tried to suck the life out of her. Mina rolled her eyes back and let them fall closed. She continued to moan from the depth of her being.

Steven and Ibra chatted incessantly. Each of their denigrating comments gave rise to another. They fed off each other's words. Their intentions became fully revealed.

"Man, I wish I could taste a piece of that right now," Steven said.

Ibra grunted and slapped Mina's rear as she wriggled.

"Not yet. You know I always go first. And you need to focus on the road. We'll see what's left of her when we arrive."

"You're right. Tell me everything you're doing to that bitch though."

Ibra played with Mina's body over her clothes initially. Stroking and prodding at her with his clammy hands. He fondled his own body aggressively, taking great satisfaction in his dominance. Unveiling all that separated him from Mina, he ripped off his shirt sending buttons to the van floor and then unzipped his pants. Ibra stared at Mina's vulnerability. His coordination became erratic. Desire burned within him to conquer her once & for all. He dripped sweat on Mina's bare chest and took pains to intently lick it off her. Mina barely breathed as he desecrated her. He growled and mounted her on the floor. Although she remained docile, he gripped her neck with one hand and firmly held her tied hands above her head. Mina gasped for air and tried to shake herself free. Seconds later, Ibra prodded her cavity with his entire manhood, desperate to feel every inch of her. His pleasure was obvious and not easily contained. Shaking violently, Ibra exploded immediately. He was self-consumed taking no notice of the tears that streamed down Mina's red cheeks.

Ibra pushed Mina's body from underneath him and then busied himself stroking the remnants of his pleasure.

"Stay there," Ibra said. "That's all you're good for anyway."

Mina lay still, near dead. Her thoughts were only of how her body had failed her. Hate ravished her body from the inside out. She was supposed to fight, but there was no fight in her; only fear.

It doesn't matter now. I'm ruined flesh. Just meat and bones. Nothing more.

She was tired and feeling closer to death than she ever felt before. Mina was only able to feel the pain and hurt that Ibra had just unleashed. She remained motionless and allowed her mind to illuminate the scene that her consciousness began to show her. What was initially hazy, came quickly into focus.

Mina's consciousness unveiled a similar scene to her present situation. She explored an unfamiliar life and time yet observed a very familiar physical body. Her consciousness allowed her to hover over this familiar yet foreign woman. Mina ruminated for a bit as she saw a face that resembled hers. The woman's features were striking and from head to toe. She was beautiful and appeared strong. Her muscle definition was impressive despite being sheathed by thin dark fabric. Her face was expressionless as she lay still, but her stillness told a tale. Mina longed to reach out to this woman who lay still on a surface underneath her.

A regal looking older man approached the woman. He raised his hands up and lowered his head. He spoke in a language that Mina did not understand and tears drenched his face as he lifted his head up.

"She's gone," he said speaking to the group of men in the room.

"Are you certain?" a young man called out from outside of the door.

"Yes. The elder has confirmed," another man said.

The elder stood over the woman's lifeless body, which was drenched in blood. He closed her eyes with two fingers and covered her face with a tattered cloth.

"She shouldn't have fought back," he said with his head cast down.

"She wasn't the kind to listen," an older man chimed in from the doorway.

"Yes. We all know, baba. Maybe she'll be obedient in her next breath," the elder said. He exhaled deeply and gently placed his hand on her forehead.

The warmth of the elder's hand translated to Mina's present state. She felt the warmth on her own forehead and the love embedded in the elder's touch. She was transfixed by this additional consciousness and her mind raced. She was certain that she had seen herself laying on the surface with her face covered in death. Many questions raced through her mind. *What happened to her and how did she end up like that?* As she searched her thoughts, her body changed. Her erratic heartbeat slowed to a steady drum beat. She returned to her current predicament, physically and mentally. She was fully present in her body and the van.

No. No.

I won't be obedient.

I will fight back.

Mina breathed in and out, loudly and deeply. Ibra did not even look her way. She let the rhythm of her breath transform her. She concentrated on the sound of her breath and the satisfying feeling it produced in her. In this state, she didn't feel Ibra's touch. She didn't feel the violation of her temple. She didn't feel the substances that dripped out of her and started drying on her thighs. She didn't feel the cords that tied her together. She felt her heartbeat. She felt her chest inflate. Her heartbeat was consistently in sync with the drumbeat in her head. She concentrated on that beat until it was all she heard. It resounded in her ears and accompanied a warmth in her belly that she was now very familiar with.

She inhaled sandalwood and felt her muscles elongate and her confidence rise.

"Do you know who you are?" she heard a whisper and felt shallow breath on her ear.

Mina opened her eyes and gazed on the silhouette of Eshu. He stood over her grinning. His essence was overwhelming for Mina but went undetected by the others.

He touched her face and rubbed the spot where the scar had appeared. He leaned in, connecting his lips to the scar and breathed into it. Steady hefty breaths filled Mina's body. Next, he cupped his hands on her groin. Internal waters flooded her cavity. The cleansing waves created a force within her. Eshu then laid his hands lightly on Mina's chest. He spread his fingers and applied pressure; it sent a shiver through her body that appeared as convulsions. The initial sensation of warmth immediately translated to freezing cold and overtook her body. Mina shook uncontrollably.

"She's seizing! Steven!" Ibra yelled.

"Turn her on her side!" he yelled back.

Eshu faded into the air that brought him.

Mina regulated her breathing and gained strength. She inhaled slowly, recognizing the coldness of ice that now coursed through her veins. As Ibra rolled her, she wriggled out of the cords that tied her but left her hands behind her back. Ibra checked her breath and leaned over her closely. Mina carefully popped the cords that bound her legs in one quick movement that went unnoticed.

Once Mina demonstrated to her captors that she had regained control of her breathing, Ibra returned her to lying on her back.

"Are we close? We gotta move this chick," Ibra said.

"We're here. I'm going to run inside for a sec. Be right back. You got her? "

"All day," Ibra responded.

Steven whistled and rolled the van to a stop. He left the keys in the ignition and stepped out.

Mina waited for Steven to shut the van door and enter the building. Once the building door closed Mina knew it was time. She bounded to her feet and lowered to a crouch. She raised her head, centered herself and stared at Ibra. She smiled showing all teeth and let out an ear-piercing yell.

"Warriors rise!" she bellowed deeply.

Without hesitation, she pounced. She sprung to his neck, grabbed him and quickly threw him to the back door of the van. The back window shattered spraying glass everywhere as Ibra's body collided with it. The van rocked with that thud. Mina kicked the van locks with her heel, securing them both inside and went back to Ibra.

Sitting on his torso with a foot at his windpipe, she slowly placed her hand on his chest. Held like a knife, she inched her hand through his skin. With consistent pressure, she kept pushing. She felt the bones of his ribcage crack. She flicked a few more times, moving impediments. He screamed out in pain. Unmoved, Mina expanded her fingers and felt around for his heart. Additional bones cracked at her hand and his chest started to cave inward. Ibra kept screaming. He yelled exasperated, as a man meeting death, but Mina wasn't moved by his agony. She leaned in to him. Her exposed breasts grazed his arm.

"Is this what it's like to be on the other side?" Mina asked. Mina wiggled her fingers as she spoke. She cocked her head and smiled.

Swiftly, she detected his strong heartbeat, and wrapped her hand lightly around Ibra's heart muscle. She pulsated her fingers around his muscle sending him into full cardiac arrest. He gasped although no air escaped his lungs. She pulled her bloody hand from his chest in a quick movement and got up, leaving him writhing on the floor. He gripped his chest and curled into the fetal position. Mina watched as Ibra's eyes rolled to the back of his head and he slipped into unconsciousness. She couldn't resist his vulnerable state and kicked him in the back repeatedly.

"Trash! That's all you're good for."

Mina didn't know if Ibra was dead or alive and didn't care. Mina pushed Ibra to the corner and sat in the available seat. Although pressed for time, Mina adjusted her clothes, knotting them and making them fit for battle. No longer dressed to the nines, Mina worked quickly to rip, tie and transform herself into a warrior. She pulled her hair back and felt under the seats for her purse. With her purse still intact, she pulled out a pair of thinly rolled ballet slippers and jettisoned the beloved stilettos that she was still wearing. She was ready and felt every bit prepared. She touched the wound on her forehead feeling the open flesh underneath it. No longer a scar, her wound bled a little.

Ibra started to moan on the floor. Filled with rage, Mina crept to him and struck him with a blow to the head that put him out cold immediately.

"I know what you did, Ibra. I know. They told me everything."

Mina paused briefly to hiss at Ibra's motionless body. She peered through the window to see their surroundings. They were parked in a large lot. Steven was nowhere in sight. There was an abandoned warehouse a few feet away. A light was on and she saw Steven's shadow inside. She executed the plan as she had rehearsed. She enabled the audio record feature on her phone and slipped it inconspicuously yet securely to her undies. It was tied in place, with no option to slip. She wore it like she was packing a gun on her hip. She stepped out the door back door of the van and crawled along the ground. In only a few paces, she reached the door and stood behind it.

Looking through the cracks, she saw Steven approaching. He swung the door open nearly hitting Mina. In one swift movement, she hoisted herself onto the door frame and delivered a striking blow to his neck followed by a number of rapid jabs to his head. With a forceful kick, Mina propelled him into the air for a few yards. Steve dropped to the ground but not before gripping his gun.

Once down, Steven whipped out his weapon and fired three shots point blank at Mina's head. Turning to the protection of the door, Mina leapt behind it. The old wooden door splintered at the collision with the bullets. Dodging bullets and seeking greater protection, Mina stepped into the path of the last bullet. She turns and ducked quickly but the last bullet connected with Mina's cheek.

"You're a coward!" Mina's deep voice boomed from behind the door.

Steven laughed uncontrollably sitting on the ground.

"What else you gonna do, Blake?" he yelled. "You know you can't do a damn thing to me. Not when I got this," he said waiving the pistol in the air.

Mina stood up straight and drew in a deep breath. She raised her voice in a blood curdling yell. Incoherent and high pitched she launched into her warrior cry. The sustained high pitch threated to destroy Steven's ear drums. He immediately dropped his gun to cover his ears.

At that, Mina ran the few yards toward him. Blood from her forehead ran down her face and into her mouth. Her eyes bulged as she yelled louder and stronger. Her sound was consistent and her breath was maintained. She seemed to have embodied an entire clan of warriors. With full strength she held her warrior cry steady, fully intending on piercing Steve's inner ear. Disoriented, Steven couldn't move.

Mina quickly reached him face to face. Snatching up his firearm, she pointed it at his forehead. Mina stopped screaming and directed him to his knees.

"Did you kill Oren Blake, Steven?" she asked slowly and deliberately.

He mumbled inarticulately.

Mina placed the barrel at his temples and cocked it. "Again, Deputy Lakos," Mina raised her voice slightly, "did you kill Oren Blake?"

Steven's body started to shake. But he did not speak. Mina dropped the gun and went after his neck with her bare hands. She felt the skin give way to her hand and she entered his body through his neck in a quick but controlled manner. She marveled at the muscles she felt around her fingers. The whites of his eyes widened as he appeared to be going into shock. She lifted his body from kneeling to a standing position.

Mina loved the power that she felt in that moment. She desired to feel life leaving the body.

She longed to feel the final moments of someone's existence. As she yearned, she heard the drumming begin. The vibration resounded within her chest.

"Don't you know who I am? I can break your neck with the flick of my finger, Steven. You don't know half of what I can do." Mina lowered her voice and her eyes to speak.

Mina felt the weight of his body as he swooned in the air. But his weight did not phase her one bit. In that moment, Steven was light. Mina wasn't sure if she was gaining strength or if her arms were being held up by a host of other arms.

"We can do this all day. So, are you going to talk to me?" Mina asked, still holding Steven's neck internally. Her speech was guttural and nearly incoherent now.

Steven groaned. Mina understood his groans to mean that he was in agreement.

In quick succession, Mina removed her hand from Steven's neck and dropped him. He doubled over coughing and wheezing. Mina slapped him on the back one time to regulate his breathing. He slumped to the ground.

Standing over his body, Mina learned down to his ear. "You kill Oren Blake?" she whispered.

"No. It wasn't me," Steven mumbled holding his neck while still doubled over.

Mina beat her chest four times and growled loudly.

"You gonna die now, Steven! All I do is one wrap. One wrap. Like this." Mina wrapped her hands in each other and demonstrated choking his neck with her very powerful hands. "Ready? Trust me, if I don't kill you, They kill you. They know what you've done, Steven."

"I swear to you. I did not kill your husband!" Steven moaned.

Mina's eyes burned with a deep crimson glow. She placed her index finger at Steven's left ear. Without much effort, she pushed. She quickly by-passed bones and cartilage. She poked quickly and Steven screamed. He doubled over holding his ear that was now gushing bright red blood.

"Then who?" Mina demanded.

"Jo-Max," Steven whispered still shaking.

"Who?" she again demanded.

"Jo-Max," he said, in between panting.

"Who hired him?" she asked.

"You and I already know," he said with a bloody smirk on his face.

"Tell me how, before I break ever bone in your ear." Mina demanded quietly yet forcefully.

Steven tried his best to remain smug, but he shook with fear as he answered. "Look. It's dangerous to interfere with another man's hustle. We place hits. That's a part of the game."

Picking up the gun, Mina knocked him in the head with his pistol, laying him out. He fell over to the side.

Unsteady on her own feet, Mina placed her hands in a prayer position and whispered something. Deep in the recesses of her mind, Mina heard the drumming fade.

At that moment, Detective Toure, Candace, and Sam screeched to a halt in the gray coupe that had clearly been speeding through the parking lot.

Detective Toure was the first to scramble out of the car and run to her side.

"Mrs. Blake, you're hurt!"

"I'm done here," Mina said collapsing to her knees.

✠ CHAPTER 42: FINALLY

Mina stretched out on the couch. She gripped a cup of tea with both hands and took sips intermittently.

"Candy! You done yet?" she called. "It's coming on soon."

"Almost. Finishing up the frosting."

"Candace, you've become a culinary genius over the last few months."

"Who knew I'd turn to the kitchen in times of stress," Candace said smiling.

"I guess now we both know." Mina tapped her stomach.

Candace emerged in her apron, wiping her hands.

"I'm going to miss this, you know."

"I know," Candace said, squeezing Mina's hand and sitting beside her.

"Who do you even know in Oyo?" Mina asked.

"Oh my God, Mina! It's amazing. Auntie connected me with Baba's family. We've been chatting up a storm online. I'm really looking forward to finding this part of me in Oyo. Can't believe I didn't tell you about it."

"Yeah, we've been busy." Mina sighed and rested her head on the back of couch.

"And tired. Don't forget tired," Candace said, rubbing her face.

"And recuperating."

"I really thought he broke my jaw, Mina."

"I know, honey. He almost did. And you know how he tried to break my spirit. He wanted to tame me, make me catatonic, teach me a lesson. I don't know, kill me? He's, he's evil." Mina stammered.

Mina had a far-away look in her eyes. Her thoughts were detached from her body and she desperately tried to distance herself from reliving that moment again. Although she had physically recuperated, her thoughts unleashed a slow- release poison that spread throughout her being. She had a few remnants of the struggle and a couple faint bruises on her body. She had healed well, but only on the outside. Mina continually rehashed how she thought her body had let her down. Ibra took her and there was nothing she could do to fix that now. Her agility and strength had not prepared her for the mental immobility that she experienced. After she had trained so hard and even tapped into her warrior spirit, her body still had allowed Ibra to do the unspeakable. She felt weak and emotionally drained. There was no coming back from that.

"What could make a man do that?" She asked Candy and shook her head. "I just don't get it. But Ibra Marcus won't be doing anything like that to anyone else. Not for now at least."

"Mina, I was sure he was dead when we showed up. What did you do to him? He's still comatose, ya know."

Mina shrugged her shoulders.

"Hell if I know or care, Candy."

"Aren't you the least bit curious if he's even alive or at least what his prognosis is?

"No." Mina said dryly.

It's crazy to me that everyone turned their backs on him so quickly." Candace said.

"Everyone but—"

"Steven Lakos," they said in unison.

"He used to be so beloved." Candace said sounding forlorn.

"He's being disbarred in addition to all the charges," Mina said matter-of-factly.

"Get out!" Candace exclaimed.

The doorbell rang. Candace jumped up to get it. Detective Toure walked in and kissed Candace on the hand. "Hi, beautiful."

"Wow. Now that's a hello," Mina called from the couch.

"Hey, Mina." The detective walked over and kissed her on the cheek.

"Hey, Toure."

Detective Toure and Candace nestled on the couch, and squeezed Mina in the process.

"It's on, you two," Mina said.

A scheduled press conference ran and was aired on every major television station.

Chief Lakos stood at a podium with a number of microphones aimed at him. He was among a few other distinguished officers and the mayor. He spoke authoritatively.

"Citizens, it is with great remorse that I share with you the outcome of the investigation into the death of Senator Oren Blake. Upon a detailed sting operation led by Detective Scott Toure and unidentified assistants, we have secured a confession of one individual who is implicated in the senator's death. Upon further investigation, there is reason to believe that this is the act of a career criminal for hire. We have even produced evidence that has since been turned over to the grand jury. Additionally, we have uncovered a dangerous new drug called SILO. There is a link between this dangerous drug and the recent missing persons and potentially the serial rape cases. I am imploring everyone to be vigilant as this drug has habitually been given to unsuspecting women who were then sexually assaulted. Our department will be investigating this further. Detective Scott Toure is heading up that task force. Other individuals have been charged in relation to the Blake case, details of which will be revealed in subsequent reports and conferences.

"Also, in light of recent transitions in our department, I will be delaying my retirement indefinitely and staying on as chief of police. Thank you. Are there any questions?"

Reporters flooded him with questions.

Detective Toure clicked off the TV.

"So, what about the missing women, Toure?" Mina asked.

He shook his head and grabbed both of their hands. "We'll have to keep looking."

"I'll help in any way I can," Mina said. "I trust my spirit."

✠✠✠✠

For more information on this work and other publications, find us at indulgentinsights.com.

To contact the author, email Shirley@indulgentinsights.com.